Wait For Me

Wait for Me

A Granite Ghost Story

RICK McGILL

ON A LATE SPRING DAY IN 1865, A PENNSYLVANIA-born prospector named Hector Horton reined his horse up a deserted draw in the foothills of the Flint Mountain Range, in what was then the Territory of Montana. He had worked his way around the West searching for gold and silver, starting in California during the Gold Rush of '49, and had several successful veins to his credit. As word of gold in Montana Territory spread among the other mining camps of Nevada and California, it eventually reached Horton's ears, and he made his way north.

That night, as legend has it, in the light of his campfire, he spied the glint of silver in a rock outcropping above his camp.

Hardly believing his luck, he pried out enough surface ore the next morning to make an assay. His experienced eye was convinced that it was worth filing a claim to begin mining the site.

First, he needed to mark the ground with the boundaries of his 1,500-foot by 600-foot claim, then get to the nearest county seat in Silver Bow, over 50 miles away, to record it at the county office. The region was sparsely populated, and the town itself held only a few hundred people. But Silver Bow was growing fast as other silver and gold strikes were popping up nearer the town. It was soon renamed Butte and it came to be known as "The Richest Hill on Earth."

The hard, mostly trackless country would take Horton four or five days to cross. During the trip, he contemplated whom to gather as investors to develop the mine and the mill that would follow. Sam Hauser, James Stuart, and Walter Dance were early contributors, as was the St. Louis & Montana Mining Company. Hauser would one day be Governor of Montana. Remember the St. Louis reference later in this story.

Soon word spread, as it always does when new veins are discovered, and silver and gold claims sprang up around Horton's original mining camp.

Originally called Camp Creek at first due to the stream that led down from the hills toward modern-day Montana Highway 1, the newborn town's name was eventually changed to Philipsburg after mining engineer Philip Deidesheimer, who designed and supervised several local mines and smelters. (Practical town managers knew that Deidesheimerburg would never work.) Deidesheimer is famous among mining historians for inventing square-set timbering, a means of shoring up large open interior spaces underground to prevent cave-ins, a process that spread internationally and saved many lives.

Philipsburg and the town of Granite, depicted in the tale that follows, are real places. One still exists. One is a ghost town. Most of the businesses and some of the historical names in this story are also real; others are fiction. I leave it to fellow history buffs to work out which is which.

To those who may deride my inaccuracies of timing or mining processes, rest assured, I've added just enough bone to the broth to make the narrative work. If this story piques your interest, the history of Granite is well worth investigating. It was the largest silver mine in the world in its day and was quite self-sufficient.

The Granite County Museum and the Philipsburg Opera House are also real, as is the local candy store mentioned in the story, the world-famous Sweet Palace. The owners of all three would love to meet you if you ever find yourself exploring old Montana.

Rick McGill
2025

IN A SMALL TOURIST TOWN OF EIGHT HUNDRED residents in western Montana, Steve and his fourteen-year-old daughter, Janie, wandered off the main town thoroughfare called Broadway and up Sansone Street. They admired the historic buildings on both sides of the street and enjoyed the summer sunshine. They'd come to explore the American West on vacation from Baltimore, and the wide-open Montana spaces and scenery were working their magic.

They chose Philipsburg when Janie wanted to see what the "real" Montana was like, not the one depicted in movies. Locals called it "The 'Burg," and it began as a mining town in the 1800s. It even boasted a respectable ghost town on the mountain overlooking the city. Granite had its heyday during the silver boom but went bust before the turn of the twentieth century.

They stopped in front of the Opera House Theater, built in 1891, and Steve consulted his local map of interesting sights.

"The oldest continually operating theater in Montana," Steve said. "Nice old place, huh?"

Janie cupped her hands up to the glass and peered inside the front doors.

"Too bad it's closed," she said. "Can we come back for the vaudeville show tonight?"

"Sure. The folks at the gem mining store said it's always a neat show," he said.

"I just wish Mom were here."

"Me, too, honey. But sometimes her patients have to come first."

Alicia Crass was an orthopedic surgeon at Johns Hopkins Hospital in Baltimore. Their vacation plans had suddenly changed when one of her patients developed complications and needed an unexpected procedure the day they were all leaving for Montana.

"She'll catch up with us in Glacier next week, don't worry." He looked up at the marquee again. "You're right, though. She loves vaudeville."

Janie groaned. "You people are so old."

As they turned away, deciding where to explore next, Janie glanced at the tall brick building across the street. It looked like an apartment house or hotel. Three stories high, the roof line held a pediment ornately inscribed, "Courtney Bros. 1918." Her gaze scanned the empty windows across the front and landed on one in particular.

"Look, Dad. There's a man watching us. Up there in that window."

In a second-floor window, they could see a man seated just inside the glass. At first, he was indeed watching them, but only briefly. Then his focus turned more up the street as if he was expecting to see something or someone coming down the road. It was hard to make out details, but he was on the senior side of life. His face looked like it held many stories—of hard times and hard work, as well as good times—all competing for expression.

"He looks like an Old West character," Steve noticed the awning over the front door. "That's the local museum, should we check it… Whoa."

The gentleman in the second-floor window suddenly vanished. He didn't get up and leave. He didn't close the shade. He didn't move at all, in fact. He just faded quickly from sight, as if he was never there.

"Did you see that? He just, like, disappeared," Janie said. She was used to all kinds of high-tech tricks, but even she was impressed.

He chuckled. "That was some pretty neat special effects. Probably draws lots of visitors."

They waited for a rickety farm truck to go by, bits of hay trailing in its wake, one more example of the "real" Montana Janie was looking for. Then they crossed the street to the museum. Steve held the door for her, and they went inside. The lobby was slightly cooler than outside—they had encountered only a few old buildings in town that actually had modern air conditioning.

To one side was a large, open meeting room, and the gift shop opposite was the actual entrance to the historic exhibits. A soft cross-breeze flowing through the meeting room and out through the lobby accounted for the comfortable temperature. An antique pump organ was displayed in the lobby, complete with Victorian sheet music on its ornate wooden rack. Old photos of buildings around town adorned the walls. A sampling of 19th-century artifacts drew their attention further in. An ornate side table held a woman's hand mirror, patinated with age, while a delicate cloth parasol stood in an intricately carved umbrella stand beside the organ.

Steve learned from his tourism brochure that this was a mining town in the old days, but more recently, the economy depended on ranching and agriculture—and of course, tourism.

They walked into the museum gift shop, where an older gentleman with wavy silver hair and a white bushy mustache sat on a stool behind the counter, reading a book. He wore an ivory-colored shirt with a stiff, old-fashioned paperboard button collar, common in the 1800s, and a dark silk vest that hung loosely on his bony frame. An old ledger was open on the glass counter, no doubt part of the museum's collection of old records and manuscripts.

He pushed his glasses back up his nose, and when he smiled, the lines in his face changed places. "Welcome to our museum, folks."

"Hi," said Janie.

Her father nodded and glanced around the shop. There were no other visitors, and it appeared they had the place to themselves. He decided to ask about the disappearing effect they had seen in the mannequin upstairs.

"How do you make that mannequin disappear upstairs?" Steve asked. "That's pretty cool."

The old man was gently closing the old ledger book, but stopped and raised an eyebrow, and cocked his head to one side. "Mannequin? Oh… Oh!" He let the ledger close with a soft thump. "You saw something? Really?"

"Yeah. Pretty authentic. Do you have it rigged like that to draw people in, or what?"

"You *really* saw him? No one sent you over to get me all stirred up?" The old man took on a suspicious tone. "Last year, Charlene at the candy store told a gal to come over and—"

Janie giggled.

"Nope. No one told us anything," Steve said. "We were waiting to cross the street just now, and that guy you have in the window did what he was supposed to do, so here we are."

The old man smiled half to himself, then leaned forward and looked at Janie.

"You saw him, too?"

Janie nodded.

"Well, first, I'm sorry for sounding suspicious. You're both nice folks, and we're glad you're here visiting our town."

The man tugged his vest down straight. "And now, second, I also have to say that was no mannequin you saw upstairs. To tell the truth, I'm a little jealous, because I've never actually seen him myself."

Janie and Steve looked at each other in puzzlement. The man seemed sane enough—and, of course, he was in charge of the museum, so he must be responsible or they wouldn't have left him on his own.

The man cleared his throat and stood up. Reaching across the glass case, he introduced himself.

"Name's Ralph. As you can see, I run the gift shop here at our museum. Nowadays they call us 'docents.'" He leaned toward Janie, wrinkled his nose. "Kind of a frou-frou title if you ask me."

Social filtering was apparently not one of Ralph's strengths.

Steve shook Ralph's hand in return, "Steve. And this is Janie. It's her summer trip, and she picked Montana. We're out here from Baltimore. We love your town—a really cool, old-timey place."

Janie shook the man's hand, too.

"So who is that guy?" she asked uneasily. "Do you mean he's a ghost?" She was unsure what to make of Ralph and what he was implying.

Ralph slid the old ledger off the counter onto a shelf. "Ah. Who is he indeed? Now that requires a full and thorough answer and cannot be rushed through. I hope you folks have some time to kill?"

Steve saw Janie's head bobbing in agreement and knew the afternoon was wide open—and apparently now decided.

At the same time, Ralph could see that Janie was calling the shots. "Well, in that case," Ralph said, "the story also requires a nice cup of tea and a comfortable chair to go with it. Why don't you both take a wander through the museum, and I'll put a pot on the cooker? Take your time while I gather my thoughts and set up a place here on the table."

He motioned toward a long reading table and chairs in the center of the shop and turned to collect a few implements of hospitality from behind the counter.

Janie and Steve headed off to the displays while the tinkle of cups and saucers on a serving tray told of Ralph's preparations.

Once they were out of earshot, Steve said softly, "He seems harmless."

Janie smiled but wasn't quite sure what to think of the implications of an actual ghost upstairs. The natural inquisitiveness of her younger years had recently developed a skeptical armor. She was ready to hear the tale but expected a logical outcome.

Steve found the museum very interesting indeed. It told of the early days of the town and surrounding area, which had its roots in the mining boom of the late 1800s. Apparently, there were some big silver mines nearby at one time, the largest named Granite, judging by the number of photos and artifacts on exhibit. There were old photos and maps, as well as old ledgers like the one Ralph had been reading when they walked in. There was even a re-creation of an old mine tunnel down in the basement, complete with tracks, a mine cart, drills, all sorts of tools, samples of silver and gold ore, and old mining memorabilia. Heavy mining machinery filled the space downstairs. Janie gaped at an exhibit of a 19th-century kitchen with a wood stove and cooking tools.

The main floor had a fascinating photo montage of some of the other ghost towns nearby. Steve surmised that this was the basis for the yarn they were about to hear.

They returned and found Ralph in the gift shop. He set a beautiful silver serving tray containing cups, saucers, and a steaming pot of tea on the reading table in the center of the room.

"So…" Ralph beamed. "How do you like our oldies-but-goodies?"

Janie said, "I can't even tell what some of those kitchen things do."

"She can cook a little, believe it or not," Steve said, "but I would hate to turn her loose in that kitchen downstairs and hope to eat anything."

Janie poked his side with her elbow.

They all had a laugh.

Ralph pointed to a few chairs at the table and brought over a plate of homemade blueberry muffins. "Make yourselves at home. I bring these from home, but most days end up eating them myself. As you can see, we're not Yellowstone or the Statue of Liberty when it comes to visitors."

He continued all the busy movements of serving a proper tea, distributing the china, spoons, and napkins, and pouring just the right amount of tea in each cup. As he set the pot back on the tray, Janie couldn't wait for the story to begin.

"So, tell us about that guy," Janie said. "I can hardly wait."

"Ah, but the waiting's the thing, young Jane." His use of her formal name got her attention, and the tone of his voice seemed to change, almost gaining a mannerism of some other place and time. He settled back.

"You see, towns come and go. Even this one will hang on someone's wall someday in faded, dusty old photographs. It's our job to remember and to pass on to others what's gone before."

He sipped some tea and shifted his gaze to the traffic passing by outside, as if searching for a place to start. Just as they began to wonder if he would start at all, he blinked once, twice, and focused again on his guests. He smiled, a twinkle in one squinting eye, and began his tale.

"I hope you inspected carefully the photos of the town of Granite throughout our museum," Ralph said, "for it is Granite that we have to thank for most of the early success of this town and the surrounding area. I won't bore you with things you can find out for yourselves on Google, just suffice it to say that Granite was a great mining city here in the 1800s, with silver and gold and lots and lots of people. Do you know how many people live in this town today? Eight hundred. And that's in summer."

He let that sink in while he took a sip of tea.

"Granite had over three thousand people at the height of its population. More lived nearby, working in the other mines and mills all over the hills above town here—some of those small mines are still working today. And all kinds of people: Italians, Chinese, Welshmen, Germans, Irishmen, Finns, you name it. You wouldn't know by visiting the crumbling ruins up the mountain now, but it was a busy place. Saloons, hotels, churches, stores, even a hospital. They had their own soda bottling company, their own ice skating rink, a baseball field…just about everything a big town needs.

"But it all depended on the mine. It was a big silver mine—biggest in the world at that time. They crushed the ore up there, smelted it into big ingots, and shipped it out by train here in Philipsburg. Millions of dollars came out of that ground. But when the price of silver crashed in 1893, well, everyone just left. The town of Granite turned into a ghost town almost overnight, they say."

"So, what about the guy?" Janie asked. "What was his name?"

A half smile crept across Ralph's lips as he settled back in his chair, nodding slowly. "Ah. His name…"

1

"NAME?"

"Jack," said the newcomer, looking around the busy office of the Granite Mountain Mining Company, hoping for a job. It was a large open space, with work tables at odd angles, desks, and shelves full of ledgers and maps. On the back wall were two large blackboards. One held figures of progress in the mine tunnels listed by date, and the other showed lists of equipment in use, out of use, and on order with expected delivery times. Two men were huddled over a large set of diagrams on a square table, carefully mapping out new sections of tunnel. Others were coming and going, shuttling folders and papers from one desk to another, delivering assay reports and ore samples. One fiddled with a coffee pot, spilling some on a big iron stove in the middle of the room—hot, sizzling streams dribbling down the side. A thin haze of cigar smoke hung near the ceiling.

After several weeks on the road—most of it with only himself for company—and now in the midst of so much hustle and bustle of the mine office, Jack failed to notice the heavyset man at the desk with his pen poised above the ledger as he looked over his glasses at Jack expectantly.

"Shall I guess your last name, mister, or just make one up for my book?" asked Tom Kelley, who was not used to being ignored by men begging for work.

Kelley was the manager for the Granite Mountain Mining Company, in whose offices Jack had arrived that morning looking for work. It was his responsibility to keep the company roster full of working men to ensure the flow of silver from the Granite mine continued to roll down the mountain.

The mine ran twenty-four hours a day, and wages were $3 for a good day's work underground. The Granite Company was a solid place to work, and more often than not, Kelley could find room for anyone who showed up looking for employment.

Anyone, that is, who could pay attention long enough to get signed up.

"Sorry, sir," said Jack. "It's Fallon. Jack Fallon. I've been on the road for a while, and your place sure seems busy to me."

He shifted his tweed snap-brim cap from one hand to the other and hoped he hadn't ruined his chances. All he owned in the world lay in a rolled-up satchel at his feet, and the few coins in his pockets would barely last another week. He had heard down in the valley that a man could find a place up here on the mountain if he wasn't afraid of hard work or the dark depths of the earth, and Jack was apprehensive of neither.

Jack was from Ireland and started working in coal mines when he was seventeen. He grew tired of the coal dust and saw what it did to his co-workers. His father died of it at age fifty, coughing and wheezing, and spitting black blood, and

Jack had no intention of joining him. He put away enough of his wages to purchase passage to America in 1889 aboard the steamer Abyssinia. He would forever love the Old Sod, but America held the promise of adventures indescribable.

When he landed in New York, the various meaningless jobs he took paid nothing compared to what his luck brought at several gambling dens once he learned cards. When he started westward, he continued to enjoy his card games and was circumspect in his winnings enough to see that being just a player wasn't the way to riches. The real money went to The House, and he fantasized about running a fine gambling house someday.

He made his way across the country by train when he could scrape together the fare. To do so, he worked an odd job now and then, just enough to live on and buy his next ticket before moving on. He landed in Chicago and stayed a while longer when his funds ran too low for the next ticket. He knocked about for a few weeks, picking up small jobs, and kept a bit of real money flowing from playing cards. Eventually, he worked for a man delivering coal by wagon far from the hubbub of the city. But coal reminded him too much of his father's demise, and he headed west once more.

It occurred to him, no matter how hard he worked, it was still for someone else. He wanted to be his own man, to work for himself and pocket the whole bit. Only then would he be in a position to settle down on a nice piece of land somewhere in his new home country and live his version of the American dream. Back in Ireland, he and his family had always been beholden to the landowners and bankers. Here, he could own his own land, and if he put enough work into it, no one could take it from him. He had seen for himself friends he knew thrown off their rented land by rich owners, and he resolved never to be like either of them—rich land-lords or the poor and homeless.

Anything and everything was possible in America. Long-range plans jostled for first place in his future. Jack entertained going into business of some kind. He could open a mercantile, or a hardware store, or a livery stable. But he knew less about horses than he did about hardware, and the more he enjoyed cards, the more convinced he became that he should build a superior saloon.

During his days alone on the road or by train, he visualized the kind of place it would be. He could see the carved woodwork of the bar, the green felt tabletops, smell the new varnish, and hear the clicking roulette wheel. He could taste the cold beer and relish never having to work for another man.

One evening in Chicago at yet another card game, a heated disagreement ensued over cheating, which Jack never did, had led to a broken nose, which he certainly did do. Unfortunately, the man's brother was Jack's boss, so his days in that vicinity were short.

Word had it there were still opportunities to be had in Montana, and a man had only to show up with all his appendages and a decent command of the English language—and at some outfits not even that—to be added to the ledger books.

Jack had heard enough in his travels westward to know he wanted to see Montana before it was all gone and citified. He had seen enough of big cities in his travels to know they were not to his liking. Perhaps he could pick up a good game of Faro there as well.

Since crossing into the state, he was convinced it was indeed a fine country. Montana held real promise. So he paused long enough to sign on for a real job with real income, and maybe put together the beginnings of his dream. His young back was as strong as the next man's, and this company looked like the right place to start.

Kelley looked the young stranger up and down and made a few quick judgments. He had intelligence behind his eyes, and it was clear he took in everything around him with the ease of someone who's worked in the dirt before. His accent was not long off the boat—a few years, perhaps. And the foreigners Kelley had known of had generally not picked up the laziness of some Americans he'd met.

"I'm no stranger to workin' or minin'," said Jack. "I've heard this is a good outfit, so I hope you can use a hand."

"Okay, Mr. Jack Fallon. Now we're getting somewhere."

Kelley took down a few more particulars, such as Jack's age—twenty-four—and his birthplace, County Kerry, Ireland. Satisfied with his first impression, he filled in the "Date Hired" column in his ledger: *May 12, 1893.*

"You go with Mr. McFeeney over there," said Manager Kelley, "an' he'll take you to a crew in the middle of their shift. Payday is a week from Friday. You can bunk in one of the company bunkhouses until then, or longer if you've a mind. You'll learn more from your fellows about what's what around here."

Kelley opened a wooden box on his desk, withdrew a metal disc stamped with a three-digit number, and handed it to Fallon. "Here's your tag. You tag in and you tag out when you come and go from the mine. Don't forget. Somethin' happens when you're underground, and we'll want to know who's down there. If you forget, even once, you're done with the Granite Mountain Company. Understand?"

"Yes, sir."

"McFeeney!"

A short, thin man with sideburns, wearing a smudged bowler hat, came over from the stove with a steaming cup of coffee. He looked a little older than Jack, but not by much. His open vest gave the appearance of someone perpetually coming or going on some urgent task.

"No, McFeeney, I have coffee of my own. See?" said Kelley. He pointed at a half-full, but cold cup on his desk.

"Take Mr. Jack Fallon here up to see Jimmy at the yard and get him started muckin'."

Fallon cleared his throat and shifted his stance. Mucking was the lowest job one could have, usually given to drifters or drunkards of little respect. It meant shoveling rocks and debris from the tunnel floor all day and cleaning up the working spaces so the "real" miners could work. With Jack's own mining past, he felt such menial work was beneath his talent and experience.

One fact he was determined not to reveal, however, was that although he had indeed worked at mining for many years, he had never been deep down a vertical shaft. He knew those boys got the best pay. Mines far apart don't check your background, so he felt safe letting Kelley assume he meant deep, hard-rock mining. Whatever got his foot in the door.

"Mr. Kelley, sir, when I said I was a miner, I meant it. No disrespect, sir, but I've worked for six years minin', and muckin's a bit under my status, if you take my meaning, is all. Again, no disrespect."

Kelley leaned forward, and his wooden swivel chair groaned under his not-inconsiderable weight. He clasped his hands together on the desk. "Mr. Fallon," he said in a low, firm voice, "and no disrespect, either, but I don't know you, and you're new in town. And it's you who's wantin' a job now, isn't that a fact?"

This was no temporary day-by-day job he was trying for. If he was serious about his future and his saloon, he would need a serious stake. Hard as it was to his pride, Jack decided to take whatever came. He knew he could make his life better with hard work alone. Fallon nodded and swallowed.

Kelley smiled. "Well, then, know this: every man on this mine started out muckin', including me. And McFeeney here. If your crew boss notices you're a good, hard worker, you'll be sittin' in this chair in no time at all." His smile instantly turned to a frown. "Now get the hell out of my office and earn yer wages."

Fallon took a step backward and nodded, putting on his cap and hefting his bag. He followed McFeeney out the door, and they started walking up the slope toward the mine yard.

Granite was built on the side of a mountain. Several streets ran more or less on a level grade, but others dipped and swerved with the topography. Every size and shape of shop, storehouse, hotel, church, and saloon imaginable lined nearly every street, shoulder to shoulder. It was hard to believe so many buildings could find a steady foundation on such slopes.

Directly across from the office was the company store, where employees could buy on credit the countless articles and personal tools they needed for work. At exorbitant prices, of course. Like most large industrial concerns, the company owned you. And the more you bought, the more indebted you became. Jack had lived that way at other mines and accepted the fact, and already knew some of the items he would need in this new job—better boots and a hat meant for mud, for starters.

"Don't worry about Kelley, mister," said McFeeney. "We get fellows up here who can't cut it, and sometimes it's a waste of time to string 'em along until they get tired of workin' and quit."

"Well, he's right: he doesn't know me. But I'm not a quitter. I might just end up in that chair one of these days." Jack grinned and shifted his pack from one shoulder to the other.

"So where you stayin'? Looks like you're livin' on the road."

"That's a fact. I thought I'd find a room before I hired on, but it happened kinda fast."

"Well, like Kelley said, you can use one of the bunkhouses." McFeeney pointed up the street at a cluster of two-story wooden barracks. "They're fine enough if all you want is a bed to sleep in. Fellows coming and going at all hours, and no liquor permitted. The Company doesn't allow spirits on any of its properties. When you get some coin, go see Elvira Headley. They have rooms to let. It's a two-story house with a green roof on the porch. Off of Bell Avenue past the old schoolhouse." He pointed again.

Jack's impression of the town was that everything seemed to be either uphill or downhill from everything else.

"Thanks. I'll look for Headley's after my shift."

The steepness of the various inclines naturally separated its neighborhoods, and seemed to indicate the social status of the residents. The Chinese section, for example, was down in a gully with small shops, houses, and shacks—as were the local brothels, of which there were quite a few, judging by the many signs for rooming houses. From his brief view down a side street, Jack saw several: *Sweetwater Rooms* and *Boarding for Gentlemen* and *$1 Haven*.

McFeeney pointed to a busy Chinese laundry on one of the flat spots near the bottom of the gully. "A man can have clean clothes every Sunday for a fair price."

According to McFeeney, who was quite the guide, Granite had seventeen saloons, several hotels, four churches, a Knights of Labor Hall, an Odd Fellows Hall, a Masonic Hall, a soda pop bottling company, its own newspaper, three mills, several mines, and a few thousand people.

The mining company owned the hospital, the bank, the mercantile, the larger businesses, and most of the lots on which homes were built. It also leased building lots in town for $2.50 per month. Those who trekked from Philipsburg and back every day soon saw the wisdom of investing in a shanty up in Granite. The local jail was tucked away in the same depression, though McFeeney explained that there was no local sheriff, and the simple one-room lockup was more for drunkards than ruffians and criminals.

As they climbed the road that led to the hoist house above the stamp mills, Jack had a better view of the working side of the town. Below him on the mountain was a massive building with a slanted offset roof, longer on the downhill side. Jack would learn it contained the seventy-stamp mill that crushed ore from the mine twenty-four hours a day. He could hear the steady rumble of the stamps dropping onto the rock, and imagined how much harder that work would be if it was done by hand. He counted himself lucky to live in such modern times, when machines relieved men from the really hard labor.

Below the mine yards was a street with bigger houses than the rest.

"The managers and highbrow folks live there," said McFeeney. "We call it 'Silk Stocking Row.' But don't worry. Most of the rest of the city is our kind of folks. We have a good share of saloons to pick from," he grinned.

The altitude alone would take some getting used to. McFeeney noticed Jack was puffing a bit as they climbed the hill, and he prepared him for a breaking-in period.

"Remember, you're up in the clouds now. In a week or two, you won't notice the air's thin," McFeeney said.

The mine buildings were a busy, confusing bunch, slapped together fast so they could get right to the business of bringing up rich ore from underground. A carpentry shop, the steam power station, and the compressor house were all built with lumber cut and milled from the local forest.

The hoist house they were headed to was on a wide shelf above the mills. It was oddly shaped, with walls taller on one side to accommodate the gallows frame, and consequently had a long, sloping roof down toward the huge steam-powered lift that lowered and raised men and ore from the depths of the mine.

A tall man in a bowler hat stood in front of the building, chewing the stub of a cigar. He turned toward them as Jack and McFeeney approached. His coat was open, and bright red suspenders framed his bulging belly. Jack was learning all he could about his surroundings and the new job. This would be his first chance to make any kind of impression on the people he would be working with. Best to keep his head down and do everything he was told so he'd be remembered as the hard worker Kelley described.

"Mr. Brownlow, this is Mr. Jack Fallon," McFeeney said. "Mr. Kelley says to put him on your gang as a mucker."

"Well, I'd be struck dead if Kelley said to start anyone other than muckin'," said Brownlow.

He looked Jack up and down, touched the brim of his hat, and nodded, dismissing McFeeney. "Come on, Fallon. Let's find you a shovel."

Without waiting for a response, he walked into the hoist house. Jack followed, ready for whatever mindless labor was to come. His outlook was, the harder he applied himself, the shorter his time at the bottom of the ladder would be.

Dominating the complex machinery in the hoist house was the main steam engine and flywheel. The crankshaft and gears were connected to a winch apparatus over the mine shaft. The lift cage was an iron frame box, open on all sides, with a railing and gate to keep its passengers inside. A sheet metal roof protected the men from falling rocks that could be jarred loose on the trip up or down. A huge drum spooled a seemingly endless flat, woven steel cable that disappeared down the shaft. Mounted on one side of the platform was a large flat circular disk with numbers around the edge, and a pointer told the hoist man the depth of the cage. The noise from the machinery precluded any attempt at conversation in the room until the lift reached its level. Then the gears thrummed down to a lower pitch and finally stopped.

When men needed to come to the surface or an ore cart was ready, the workers underground would tug on a rope connected to a bell at the hoist man's station. A large sign posted at each stop showed the specific series of bells that told the operator where to send the cage. It was all very organized and scientific.

The operator, a man in a brimmed hat and a bit cleaner clothes than other men coming and going at the mine, sat on a raised platform at the controls of the lift. He waved as Jack and Brownlow entered the open space below the operator's station.

Brownlow leaned close to Jack and spoke over the din. "You can start in here. Shovel and broom-clean by—" he drew a pocket watch from his vest—" four o'clock."

Jack nodded.

"And don't talk to the hoist man! You'll be fired if you distract him. It could kill somebody. Understand?"

Jack nodded again, and Brownlow walked out with a wave to the hoist man.

Jack judged it was before noon, though he had not heard nor seen any mention of lunch. He had skipped many meals on the road, but it was more important to give the impression of a hard worker than of one who lived by his belly. He knew he would at least have a sizable shift of hours on his first day, which meant his earnings would start off well.

Already, he was calculating how to live cheaply and set aside a fair stash to invest in his future: The Green Isle Saloon. Grandiose titles for his gambling house came and went as he made his way west; this week it was The Green Isle.

He picked up the battered and well-worn shovel, set his pack down in a corner, and commenced straightening up the floor of the hoist house. Dirt and rocks, and trash of working men littered the big room. As he worked, Jack was impressed by the massive wooden timbers that supported the building and the headframe of the hoist. To his young eyes, it was hard to imagine trees that thick, let alone the milling required to cut them into square beams. The mine cage came and went several times, bringing ore to the surface, and more spillage for Jack to clean up.

When he was working closest to the shaft itself, Jack could feel the soft upward rush of air pushed ahead of the ascending cage. It smelled of rock dust and dampness, mixed with sweat. He imagined how it must be to work far down below in that air. He looked forward to earning his wages as part of a crew, but not living like a rat in a hole forever.

The swinging doors of the Green Isle kept him focused.

It'll be worth it in the end.

It took the better part of the day to get it cleared to a point that Jack felt comfortable taking a breather outside. He stepped out and wiped his brow. A man, seeming in no particular hurry, walked up from below, the same way Jack and McFeeney had come that morning. He stopped near Jack and paused to roll and light a cigarette. He wore a floppy slouch hat, typical of most miners, a once-clean, unbuttoned coat with layers of dust and dried mud, and tall muckers' boots. The freshly lit cigarette hung smoldering under his bushy mustache like a dynamite fuse.

He stuck out his hand to Jack.

"Herman Mefling."

"Oh." They shook hands. "Jack Fallon."

The man blew smoke out of his nose, looking at the sky.

"Winter's about done, eh? Most all the snow has gone, but I wouldn't be surprised if we didn't get one more snowfall before June."

Jack reminded himself that he was now living on a mountain and snow was common late in the year. By way of small talk, this Mefling was gauging the new man. Jack had no idea of the man's position in the scheme of things, but he was cordial and agreed with the man's assessment of the prospects on the weather. Jack had worked in mines all his life and knew this fellow was gauging the new man. It was nothing personal—simply a way to know whether a man was reliable, if you'd care to share a drink after a shift, or whether you'd risk your life to pull him out of a cave-in.

"So, what's your job like? Down below," Jack asked.

"Pipefitter. Same pipe. Different day."

Jack was beginning to feel he should get back inside and back to work when the man flipped his butt away, ending the break for both of them.

"Back to work for me. Union meeting tomorrow night. See you there?"

"Oh, I'm not a member yet," said Jack.

Herman laughed.

"You are, my friend. You just don't know it yet."

They both entered the building, the clanking hoist machinery blotting out any further conversation. Herman climbed into the cage for the return trip underground.

The hoist man tilted his chin questioningly to Mefling, who said, "Eight hundred foot level, if you please, Jimmy."

With a wave to Jack, he was lowered into the shaft. The cage disappeared from sight, and the gently vibrating ribbon of steel rolled endlessly off the drum. The hoist man held the levers and brake, gauging the descent by the calibrated dial in front of the platform. As the pointer crept closer to the number "8," the hoist man tugged on the brake handle, smoothly adjusting the speed of the cable to a slow stop right at the 800-foot marker.

Jack tried to imagine the distance underground to eight hundred feet, comparing it to a stretch of railroad track, but it was difficult to picture. When Jack hired on, the main pit at the Granite Mountain Mining Company, named the Ruby Shaft, was already 1,500 feet deep. He tried not to dwell on it and hoped that his first trip down the hole wouldn't reveal his secret. If he had a sudden attack of nerves on his first descent into the shaft, it would no doubt be his last.

2

IT TOOK PARTICULARLY HARDY MEN TO GO INTO the depths looking for riches, and Jack always counted himself as one of them. But some of those tough, swaggering miners could be superstitious. Jack had heard the tales in other mines. The quiet, pitch-blackness of a deep mine, when the workings stilled at the end of the day or paused between shifts, is enough to unnerve many a hard-rock miner. If the already-dim Davy lights go out, and nearby candles are extinguished in a gust of air, and he's left alone in the deafening blackness, many's the man who has heard the soft knocking, barely audible, at the edge of consciousness.

Miners' lore told of small, mischievous creatures who sometimes lured men to their death, or were heard tapping on deep mine timbers, signaling an imminent cave-in. The Tommyknockers were spoken of, but only outside in the open air.

Jack attributed the stories to crazy Englishmen with whom he had little patience anyway. If anything, he might be tempted to knock on a mine timber himself, just to put a scare into one of the fellows working alone. But he hedged his bets and wasn't willing to tempt the possibility of their existence. He also knew pranks can be deadly in dangerous jobs, and if he got fired for childish jokes, it would only delay his plans to build the finest gaming house in the country. Young enough to feel invincible, he was old enough to keep on a steady course.

He was determined to work his way up the pecking order. He knew how mining companies worked, though this one was much larger than any he had been part of before. Do what you're told, and don't complain. That's how to get ahead.

The way McFeeney described the company rooming house, it might be better than nothing as long as the roof kept the rain out. He had slept on the ground almost all the way here, so the company house would suffice until he got his bearings. With the money he saved by sleeping in the company's house, Jack looked forward to a little jingle in his pocket, so he might afford a card game. Mining was his job, but cards were the fun of life. Poker was popular, but Jack preferred Faro, all the rage in the American West.

But if he could find it after his shift, he decided to look up the Headley house, just to see what it might cost for a more permanent lodging. His thoughts on where to sleep were interrupted when one of the workers walked into the hoist room from outside carrying a heavy steel drill bit on his shoulder. Dressed like most of the other miners, with layers of dried mud, it was hard to tell all the strangers apart. There was no mistaking the jagged diagonal scar across his face, however, and Jack kept to his cleaning duties.

While the man waited for the hoist to come up, he noticed Jack watching the machinery.

"You like our operation?" the man asked Jack. He had a slight accent—Scandinavian, possibly, but his English was fluent.

"It's a big company, to be sure," Jack said.

"You're new, I guess." He shifted the five-foot-long drill bit and rested the tip on the floor. "Good to see a young man come on. You remind me of another young fellow, came on last year. First day on the job, he was riding the cage coming up, and curiosity got the better of him."

"How so?"

"He leaned out of the cage a bit on the way up, just to see how far they were. The rock edge of the shaft knocked him down and took his head right off."

Jack had no reply, but he filed it away under lessons learned the hard way.

"Yep. A real mess," the worker said.

The cage arrived, the man tipped his wide-brimmed hat, shouted his destination to the hoist man, and returned to the depths.

Whether the tale was true or not, Jack had no way of knowing. *They probably tell stories like that to break in the new boys.*

Jack passed the entirety of his shift without speaking to the hoist man, nor had the man spoken to Jack or anyone else as they came and went. Each time, they called out their intended level, and the man sent them on their way down.

By the end of his shift, though no one actually came to tell him it was over, Jack felt he had put in a good first day of work that no one could find fault with. He had mucked the hoist house and the adjoining workrooms, as well as the surrounding yard, in royal fashion. He had helped wrestle more than a few ore carts off the lift as they came to the surface, but kept to his own job overall. Even the hoist man looked around the area and gave a nod of approval when he was done.

Jack could tell that his day was over as working crews changed. Men he had begun to recognize as they came and went all day departed, most with lunch pails in hand, and strangers arrived to take their place. The steam whistle on the outside of the building signaled the actual shift change, and he gathered up his belongings.

He went down into the town in search of Headley's Boarding House. He wandered the few streets he had passed on his way up to the mine that morning, but finally asked directions at a mercantile on a secondary street called Bell Avenue. He learned he was close to his destination and would have found it had he kept walking downhill.

When he arrived, he climbed the steps to the door and rang the bell. The woman who answered was Mrs. Headley herself. She was in her fifties and had kind eyes, with a slightly mischievous curl in her lips. She had seen every kind of miner and transient come and go, as well as some of the troubles they could bring with them.

She gave Jack the house rules: No whiskey and no women. Be considerate of your fellows who might be day sleepers. It was her roof and her door, and while you're under the first, you'll abide by the rules or use the second. She was amenable to letting Jack have a room on credit until his first payday, which surprised him, but he jumped at it. It was a company town, and anything that supported the company and its employees, new or not, was always good for business in the long run.

He offered to pay what he could now, but when she saw the small bit of money in his hand, she was inclined toward generosity. She did, however, ask to see Jack's metal mine tag to prove his employment.

Mrs. Headley showed him to an empty room and left him to settle in. He dropped his dusty pack on the floor beside the bed and took in his surroundings. There was one bed, one side table with a pitcher and wash bowl, one chest of drawers with an oil lamp on top, and a worn stuffed chair. Perfect.

He had every intention of living lean and saving every last penny. With luck, his savings would soon be difficult to conceal. He saw a bank on the main street coming into town; the Hyde-Freychlag Bank, it said on the glass front window. He resolved to start putting his cash there instead of trying to hide it in his room. A robber could search the entire place in two minutes.

3

THE NEXT SHIFT WAS NOT QUITE AS UNEVENTFUL as his first. Jack was still assigned to cleanup chores at the hoist house, but midway through the morning, he sensed a distant rumble down the shaft. He could tell by the demeanor of the hoist man and the few men who were coming and going at the time that something momentous had happened. A cave-in had happened; men down below rushed to help, but one rode quickly to the surface with the news and to summon the company doctor.

Soon, an anxious crowd of men gathered at the top of the cage hoist. Word spread that a miner was on his way up the shaft with horrendous injuries. A raise—an opening in the rock from one level to another—had suddenly collapsed, crushing a man who was now clinging to life, and, no doubt, praying for death to take him.

All were hushed in the hoist house. The only sound was the groaning cable and rumble of the gears bringing the cage to the surface.

As the top of the cage cleared the shaft, Brownlow shouted, "Stand back! Let Dr. Brandt forward!"

The cable spool groaned to a stop, and the operator engaged the brake. Men held hats in their hands while the doctor, a middle-aged, handsome man with close dark hair and a thin mustache, stepped to the stretcher still in the cage.

From his place at the back of the crowd, Jack could see that the miner's injuries were catastrophic. The parts of him that weren't covered with wet mud were obviously misshapen under his clothes, and some were bloody. His hat was gone, most everyone underground wore some kind of head covering, and his face and head showed the most blood. His torso looked quite uneven, more like a lumpy sack of potatoes where it should be smooth.

Dr. Brandt checked the man's labored breathing. There was little sign of life in his eyes: Brandt's long experience told him the man would not survive.

"You'll be okay," he told the boy, more to help relieve his anguish than to be truthful. "Take the stretcher outside!" he ordered the men closest to the cage.

Four of the miners gathered around and lifted the man and basket as one, and carried him out to be placed in the flatbed of a freight wagon with low wooden sides, normally used for hauling supplies. The wagon was frequently called to duty as an ambulance to transport injured miners down the hill to the well-appointed two-story company hospital. Once the stretcher was in place, Brandt climbed into the bed of the wagon to be with the wounded man, while another walked beside the horse with the bridle in his hand to keep close control. The trip was slow to avoid jostling the patient, tempered by the urgency of the mission.

Dr. Robert Brandt was the town and mine company doctor. He had received his medical training in the U.S.

Army and applied his skills at Army outposts across the frontier before settling in Granite. The Indian uprisings, so common in the late 1800s, gave Army doctors a constant supply of patients on whom to practice their craft.

The wagon crunched to a stop at the receiving doors of the hospital, located on the narrow end of the building closest to the street. There were three cement steps as well as a formed ramp leading up to a wide porch. The double doors were already propped open. Dr. Brandt's wife, Jillian, who was the only nurse, came out to meet them. She was a strong and striking woman of twenty-four with full blonde hair done up in a conservative Gibson Girl style.

Jillian had been born and raised in Philipsburg and had never travelled farther than Granite, four miles up the mountain. She met Brandt when he took over the hospital in 1884, and they were married later that same year by Reverend Joseph Thomas in the town's Methodist Church. She was among the short list of pretty women much talked about in town, and McFeeney, always the Scot, said she was "tidy," but none of the burly workers had ever dared anything more than wish. After all, their lives might depend on the doctor one day.

Several of the miners had accompanied the wagon down from the hoist house, like pallbearers, to give aid and support to their friend. A hospital orderly, Wallace Coates, hurried out the door to help Dr. Brandt and Jillian carry the man into the admitting room, the first stop for all patients when they arrived. It held a heavy work table on which to place unresponsive victims, as well as cabinets with bandages and medicines. Counters held the necessary accouterments for tending to medical emergencies.

Once he was moved onto the table, they removed most of his clothing, which was covered in dust and dirt from the cave-in. Brandt bent over the treatment table.

"Halt the noise!"

He used his stethoscope to listen to the man's chest. The poor fellow had not opened his eyes, nor made a sound, since being brought to the surface. The cuts and scrapes on his body revealed massive impacts from falling rock. Portions of his abdomen had indentations from the heavy boulders, which had not refilled to their normal state. His left leg was bent at an unnatural angle, the foot almost backward.

The miner's rasping breath slowed and hitched a few times, and finally ceased altogether. Brandt pounded on the man's chest once, twice, three times, and listened again, but heard nothing more from lungs or heart.

He turned to Jillian, who had seen mine accidents end badly before. Recognizing the look on Brandt's face, she looked at a large, plain clock on the wall and recorded the time of death in a ledger on the side table. Coates slowly unfolded a white sheet from a cupboard and neatly covered the body until the man's family could be summoned to collect his remains.

"What is his name?" asked Jillian, her pen poised over the ledger after writing the date and time. Then she said, "I mean, 'was.' What was his name?"

"I forgot to get it before we left the shaft," Brandt said, his face flush. Only Jillian was close enough to see his face redden, and she knew he was always hard on himself for overlooking any detail.

One of the miners who helped bring the man in spoke up from the doorway. "Halloran."

Jillian turned to him.

"Joe. His name is Joe Halloran," he said.

Jillian made the proper notation. Coates volunteered to locate the man's wife, but two of the men outside were friends of the family, and they hurried off to fetch his wife.

Brandt sent Coates on horseback to fetch Doctor William Ray, the coroner down in Philipsburg, four miles down the mountain. Although the accident was witnessed by several miners, and all agreed the rock just gave way and no one was at fault, a proper reporting of the death must be made. The coroner would determine the proper and legal cause of death to rule out foul play and maintain official records.

As the others filed out, Jillian and the doctor were alone. She turned to start cleaning up the room, but Brandt suddenly grabbed her by the arm and pulled her close. They were alone in the room with the deceased man.

"Why must you insist on embarrassing me in front of others?" Brandt hissed

She was caught off guard but had remembered his expression when he admitted his oversight regarding the man's name. A trivial oversight, to be sure, but it triggered his embarrassment. "What do you mean? I did no such thing. I'm sure it was hectic at the mine. It was more urgent that he get here to the hospital. If he could be saved—"

She tried to pull away, but his grip tightened.

"I did not ask this man's name because it was a confusing scene at the mine shaft. But you simply had to bring attention to my lapse. I have told you before to keep your criticisms to yourself!"

He turned her arm loose and leaned close to her face. "Do not cross me, Jillian."

He turned to the wash basin and cleaned the dead man's blood off his hands. He left Jillian without another word to take care of the man's personal things and prepare to receive the family.

She was too shocked to respond further, nor would she have. They had grown apart in recent years. Though Robert and Jillian were still husband and wife, working together, there were often times when he treated her no differently than he would an employee. In their early years, the treatment was more forgiving, even deferential, and they made a good medical team. Now, she felt less respected.

Recently, their relationship had cooled. From all appearances, they led a happy and full life, albeit without children. They attended church and social events together, though they quickly parted to mix with friends. Small towns are rife with rumors and whispers, of course, and the consensus was that the good doctor returned from the war unable to fulfill that particular prescription. Working side by side in the hospital was the closest they physically came to each other these days. He acted more the domineering doctor in charge than any kind of husband.

Jillian made excuses for his worsening behavior, telling herself that he was working too hard.

Of course he is overworked. This is a mining town, and one doctor could not possibly tend to so many patients.

Sometimes she felt that it was her own fault for expecting too much out of life, but lately she was believing it less and less.

Other doctors had come to work and live in Granite—come and gone, practicing their healing arts at the company hospital, and for one reason or another, eventually moving on. Her husband was the latest medical professional in charge.

There was no mistaking that Jillian loved her husband, as much as love had been taught to her growing up, and a woman's job was to support her husband through life's trials, no matter what. Her mother had set a fine example, and she tried to do the same.

But it was not a happy life. Deep in her mind, she felt there must be something more that she was missing out on in that wide, wonderful world beyond her little community that she read about in her books. Something she might find if she only had a glimpse of some larger horizon.

4

THE DOCTOR HAD BLOOD ON HIS SHIRT AND COAT, and left the examining room to go upstairs and change clothes. It was mostly an excuse to get away from other people for a few minutes. Losing a patient was nothing new, especially one as hopelessly injured as the Halloran fellow. But he internalized the failure as his own. Disease and natural deaths were commonplace in rural hospitals, but violent death always took him back to his Army days.

The Army Medical Department did not require it, but most doctors would do their best to also treat wounded Indians if they came into their care. However, it was rare for a wounded enemy to survive long enough to reach the safety of a field hospital, as soldiers often avenged the death or brutalization of their comrades.

How any man could survive such experiences without it affecting his psyche is beyond expectation. For one to become a civilian and live a happy, married life in a quiet Montana town would challenge even the gods.

When Brandt left the Army, he came to Granite and worked in the company hospital, treating injured and sick men, helping them return to work in the mines. He had become accustomed to frightening wounds from the battlefields and was undaunted by the various ways in which men were mangled by mining and its machinery. The only difference between wartime wounds and industrial injuries was that the latter were accidental—not inflicted in battle.

While experienced in medicine and utterly devoted to Jillian, Brandt at times had his dark side. Again, no one questioned it, marking it down to the wars in his past that wounded him on the inside. He was a good, competent doctor and helped many an injured miner or sick child back to health.

On the outside, both the Brandts seemed quite happy and comfortable together. But in the privacy of their apartment on the upper floor of the hospital, there were often heated accusations and complaints that Jillian bore in silence, believing it better to let Robert's mood subside on its own than to try and defend herself.

He was insanely jealous at times when he perceived Jillian was nursing her charges with more care than he thought deserving. It was totally unfounded, of course, and she was nothing but a faithful wife, if for no other reason than she feared the consequences of straying.

In her depths, she would cry into her pillow that they were trapped in a place she longed to leave behind since she was in her teens. She might have been satisfied living a small-town life, but as a young girl, she loved to read, and what she lacked in personal experiences was more than compensated for by the tantalizing images of "anywhere else."

At first, she believed marriage would bring happiness no matter where she was, but as years went by, she felt more

imprisoned in the city of Granite. If she could just find a
reason for them to move to a new town, it might even help
Robert become a loving husband again.

She was terrified to broach the real reason for her discontent to Robert—their lack of children—which, in her
mind and upbringing, was the only reason for living. But
as tensions worsened between them, she felt blessed not to
have the complication of a child. As much as she hoped to
be a mother someday, Jillian knew this was not the home to
raise one.

In the end, they had reached an uneasy peace: outwardly,
the happy couple, but inside the home, happy only to keep
from breaking the dishes.

5

MEN WHO VENTURE INTO THE DEPTHS OF THE Earth know the risk when they sign on. They also know their brothers will look after their wives and family if they don't survive a shift down below.

Joe Halloran's wake at the Miners' Union Hall that Saturday was a grand party. The three-story brick hall with stone and wood accents, built and dedicated in 1890, was the centerpiece of most social events in town. Stained glass borders surrounded the windows in front. The ground floor held a saloon and billiard tables. Dances, parties, and of course, wakes, were held in the large second-floor auditorium.

The Union Hall was filled with friends, family, and strangers hoisting their glasses to "Good Joe, the fine man." Jack hadn't been to a good Irish wake since leaving Chicago, and it became immediately clear that the Irish, as well as the Finns, Italians, and Welshmen in Granite, knew their business when it came to sending the departed off on a fine journey into the hereafter.

Jack wasn't a socialite by any definition, but he realized at once that this was his first real opportunity to interact with a wide range of people, some of whom might eventually be contributors, willingly or in a more roundabout way, through a game or two of cards, to his entrepreneurial dreams.

Typical of Irish wakes, games and hijinks accompanied the storytelling surrounding the departed. By the time Jack climbed the stairs to the second-floor dance hall, a stout game of Hide the Gulley was already in progress. In this case, the Gulley was one boy's prize pocket knife, surrendered on condition of its safe return, to a redheaded fellow who hid it somewhere in the hall while a man named Kearney, one of Jack's shift-mates, was blindfolded. His friends then steered him this way and that as he hunted and asked for clues to its whereabouts. Aside from the fun of the hunt was the reaction of people not involved in the game when Kearney tried searching back pockets and ladies' hats. Adding to the other players' amusement were his hurried explanations to avoid fisticuffs.

"Good Joe" wore his best suit in a freshly carpentered casket, newly arrived from Baskin's & Son in Philipsburg down in the valley. Tomorrow, Joe would be interred down in the Philipsburg cemetery because the largest level ground in Granite was reserved for a more important activity: the baseball field.

Jack made his way through the singing crowd to pay his respects to Good Joe's widow, a not unattractive woman of middle years, dressed in all black, of course. Her thick brown hair was pulled back into a tight bun. She was cordial but somber, and before people started arriving, she had accepted a stiff shot of whiskey from the bartender in the hall. But only one, followed by a few leaves of mint. Her mostly expressionless face belied thoughts of the days to come. She now had an uncertain future in town. Mining companies rarely paid a death benefit, and the benevolent gift from the Granite Miner's Union wouldn't last. Her only son had gone off to the Army and got himself killed fighting Sitting Bull. Friends would have to help as best they could until she could find some kind of employment. Such was the life of a miner's wife.

Jack made his way through the crowded room to the bar, cutting between a few lads engaging in a hearty slapping game, and was nearly drawn into an out-and-out brawl until he realized the slappers were in fact only playing. Such a game was always accompanied by the generous application of alcohol, as it helped the boys continue far beyond a sober man's tolerance and ensured they remained friends afterward, no matter who won.

Once he had a pint of Silver Spray, the Philipsburg-brewed beer, in hand, he made the rounds, visiting with the few friends he had made since arriving the month before. One of the tipsier attendees was Tim Kearney, who had quit the Gulley game. He was a little older than Jack, and the two had become fast friends. He knew his way around the tunnels, and Jack was still learning the ropes, although he had yet to be assigned work down below.

Tim collared Jack in the crook of his arm and drew his ear close.

"Jack, my boy, there's to be a game of Faro Monday night at Rosemary's," he said with a mischievous grin. "Clancy and me are gatherin' at eight o'clock. There's a couple of new boys just in from Fort Benton by train who might need to be educated on the Granite version of the rules, eh?"

Cards had been the impetus behind Jack's hasty departure from Chicago. He and a few of the boys had played a few small games of Faro in recent weeks, but it had been many months since he had tried his hand in a real, formal game with a full complement of players.

"Tim, if you say it's to be a fair game, I'm in. But I've no wish to pick a fight with strangers."

"Nonsense, Jack. 'Tis a fair game and that's a fact." Tim winked and wheezed a rheumy, whiskey-tinged cough. "We'll see you at Rose's at eight."

Jack nodded and drifted away through the crowd, hoping his card skills hadn't grown rusty. Short games with friends were nothing compared to the mental gymnastics of the real thing.

He knew Tim and the Clancy fellow, sure enough, but riverboat gamblers had always given him pause. They drift in and out of towns, knowing no one, and asking to be trusted as strangers. He hoped Tim and Clancy would jump to his aid should he find himself on the winning end of a questionable hand.

The wake continued through the night, and on Sunday morning, those who could still stand, along with those who had regained consciousness in time, accompanied the widow and the funeral hearse down the mountain to the Philipsburg Cemetery for Good Joe's final act.

Jack was not present.

Though not a teetotaler, Jack's priority was to be fit enough for his shift at the mine on Monday morning. He had left the wake just after ten and made his way through the hilly streets of the darkened town to his room at Elvira Headley's boarding house. The brisk air and walk cleared his head, and he thought about the coming card game. His strategy of sobriety, and sometimes-feigned drunkenness, had never failed him.

One rainy night gambling in a Chicago saloon, he'd chosen his drinks as carefully as his bets, and was quite a bit more sober than his opponents. Consequently, he was also winning quite a bit more than they.

By the time Jack decided to take his leave, two other players had determined—mistakenly, of course—that Jack had been cheating them and proposed to settle things in the street. Jack made quite a mess of the table and chairs in the tiny bar as he made a hasty retreat through flailing fists and jabbering gamblers.

As he ran down the street into the fog, a shot rang out and a bullet hissed by his head. Jack's feet barely touched the cobblestones as he disappeared into the night.

Now he wondered if he was about to replay the entire affair with a different cast of characters, at a much higher altitude. Jack was no coward and knew the game would commence as promised, but he was no fool, either. He planned to be on his best behavior and hoped his new friends would watch his back.

As he climbed the steps to the boarding house, he saw that the lamp was still lit in the parlor. Jack quietly let himself in, but was met by Mrs. Headley in the hall.

"Mr. Fallon, I hoped you wouldn't be another one of my 'cases' to keep an eye on."

"No, ma'am," said Jack. "Tonight was the wake for one of the fellows. I promise you, I've had nothing more than a beer. Just to be social, you understand. I surely don't get into my druthers."

She nodded and softened. "Well, a wake then. And it's not yet 11 o'clock." She smiled. "I knew you were a good boy. I'll wait 'til you're up the stairs to put out the lamp, then. Goodnight, Mr. Fallon."

"Yes, ma'am. Goodnight to you."

Jack headed up the stairs to his room and knew he had just passed the test. His landlady had no patience for trouble and was waiting up for him to see if her first impression of him was right.

It was.

6

THROUGHOUT HIS SHIFT ON MONDAY, JACK KEPT thinking about the evening to come. He had been careful to set aside as much cash as possible every payday to live on, plus a little extra for cards. He carefully budgeted his "playing money" in the few small games he had played with friends, mostly to keep in practice. This was the first opportunity to really let his card money run, and if luck favored him, it could add substantially to his nest egg.

But work came first, and he was finally assigned a shift underground. That meant he had to make his first-ever trip down the shaft on that long steel cable. He had graduated from mucking the mine yard to mucking the mine face—the actual working end of the tunnel. Charges of dynamite chewed into the mountain a few more feet each shift, and Jack would be filling ore carts with blasted rock and dirt all day long. Basically the same job he'd done since he was hired, only now he'd be doing it hundreds of feet below the surface of the Earth.

Keeping to his far-ranging plan, if he could stay with this outfit over the coming winter and keep finding ways to advance his position, Granite might be his big win. The work was no problem. He accepted orders from his bosses willingly and could tell that they were noticing he was a steady worker.

His only apprehension was this first trip straight down.

In the back of his mind, he knew he would have to face it sooner or later. The horizontal drifts he had worked in his prior jobs were nothing compared to straight down into the pit. As he waited his turn in line with the other men, each step brought him closer to that black hole. He could feel the cold air welling up from the ground and smell the dank rock and mud. Granite was a "wet" mine, and water continually seeped in everywhere. Steam-powered pumps kept the tunnels clear enough to work in, but mud was a fact of life.

Jack stepped into the cage, and the gate, just an iron bar, clanged shut on him and six of his fellows. He resisted the urge to grab onto the railing, though he was surrounded by men on all sides anyway, and would have to stretch past one of them to reach it. Jack happened to be facing Tim Kearney, who was oblivious to Jack's discomfort.

The cage lurched and began its slow dive into the dark. Jack inhaled deeply and quietly, so as not to reveal his anxiety. One of the men carried a Davy lamp and lit it as the daylight receded, so they had a bit of illumination for the journey down the shaft.

The Davy Safety Lamp was unique to mining work. It was about the size of a typical oil lantern but contained the burning wick safely behind a wire mesh to prevent an explosion in the presence of flammable gases.

The cooler air rushing from the pit had been an illusion. The deeper Jack went, the warmer it got. Rock near the surface cooled the warmer air rising from the bottom. As they descended, Tim shed his shirt and remained bare-chested for his shifts. Some of the other men talked among themselves.

Jack leaned into Tim and spoke quietly. "It's not so bad."

"What isn't, Jack?"

"Going down."

Kearney cocked to the side with a confused half smile.

Jack finally confessed, "Between you and me, Tim, and if you tell anyone, I'll have your teeth, but this is my first trip down a shaft in my life."

Kearney said nothing, but his lips made a tight, pursed circle that turned to a grin. He only nodded but kept his thoughts to himself. *Wait 'till I tell the fellows, teeth or no, our Jack's a virgin!*

Jack spoke quietly so only Tim could hear. "I've done plenty of mining, but none of them were like this—straight down. It's just that, well, I heard some companies pay a little extra for the men who actually work down in the tunnels."

Tim patted Jack on the shoulder, having a good but quiet laugh at Jack's expense.

"That's a fine idea, Jack-O. Why don't you bring it up at the next union meeting?"

Just then, the cage slowed and came to a stop. This work today took him to the 700-foot level. Jack and Tim stepped off and got to the task at hand, filling more carts with ore nearly two hundred feet back in the tunnel. The spoils they were clearing had been blasted during the previous shift and left to sit while the dust and powder fumes settled. Once he got used to working in the much darker confines of the tunnel, it felt more like his previous jobs, and Jack applied himself to the work; his anxiety at being so deep disappeared. Work was work, and dark was dark—deep or shallow, it was all the same. Memories of Joe Haloran's battered body being lifted off the cage were forced from his head, and Jack felt he would stick with the Granite company as long as he could.

With only some nearby lamps that barely gave enough light to work, it was easy to dismiss his proximity to Hell itself despite the heat. At least his job did not require much concentration, leaving his brain to wander back to the Faro table while his back strained at the drudgery.

Later in the day, as he and Tim awaited another empty cart to roll to the mine face for them to fill, there was enough time to grab a bite to eat.

"What's in your pail?" Jack asked.

Tim shrugged his bare shoulders, glistening with sweat. "Pasty. Now what else do you think I'd bring down here, Boy-O? A steak dinner from the Metro?"

The Metropolitan Hotel was the city's highbrow eatery, famous for local steak, though none of the miners could afford to partake of its menu.

Jack chuckled. His lunch pail was something to look forward to at mid-shift. It, too, contained a pasty, freshly baked that morning at Headley's. Residents could pay a little extra to have a hot meal ready to go into their pail, which was owned and loaned by Headley's.

Although it was made of sturdy metal, the rats had learned to open more than one unlucky man's pail by knocking it off a ledge. Jack had been lucky not to battle rats working on the surface. Now he followed the example of older, experienced men and kept his food safe. Meals were eaten at the work space down in the shaft, as one or two men at a time would take a breather and wolf down whatever the rats had left them.

A water wagon made its way up and down the tracks and Jack and Tim forced down as much as they could drink. The heat took its toll, and the men hated the sloshing warm water in the tank. A cold beer it wasn't, but the alternative meant lost wages if someone succumbed to dehydration.

Experienced men watched out for the new boys, but Jack made a good first impression on his shift mates and was no longer considered new. He had learned long ago the feeling of acceptance that eventually came from strangers on a new job—not in words specifically, but in the way they acknowledged your ability, or not needing things explained in detail like a new man did.

The water wagon was one example when Jack needed no urging to partake. He had once been in dire straits, many years before. As a younger miner, he had once been carried out after skipping too many visits from the wagon, and that was a mistake he pledged never to repeat. He took his turn when the wagon came, regardless of the taste, and the others noticed.

The company, any mining company, went to great lengths to keep men at their positions working all through a shift. The length of time out of a shift to ride the cage up to the surface and back down again for trivial things like meals, water, or other functions was eliminated by ensuring men stayed down in the tunnels.

With so many men working under the ground for so many hours in a day, there was also a need for an organized disposal of "waste other than sweat."

When Jack first made his way to his workspace from the lift that morning, taking in all his new surroundings, he noted that portable latrines were parked at strategic points throughout the labyrinth of stopes and drifts. Miners called them "thunderboxes," an apt description considering the echoes of rock tunnels. Usually, they were left in an unused side tunnel near the vertical shaft to limit the putrid cloud that permeated the vicinity, depending on when they were last emptied—another distasteful duty reserved for the most junior of the muckers. Jack was again eternally thankful that he was an experienced miner.

By the end of his shift, Jack had come to several conclusions. Deep mining wasn't the nightmare he expected. His concentration on the physical labor, no matter how mindless, kept him from worrying about the tons of rock above his head. And he had found a home, at least as long as he kept his record clean and produced as much as the next man. While shoveling ore into a cart, he imagined he was shoveling money into his bank account.

7

THE EVENINGS IN GRANITE COULD BE COOL, NO matter the time of year. As Jack made his way down Broadway Street toward the saloon district, he was thankful for his old wool coat that had seen him through many adventures. Smoke drifted through the night air as a few residents warmed up their homes with a wood stove, even on this summer night.

The shops were closed up and dark, but lights shone in most of the second-floor living quarters. Even though the bustle of the main street had quieted, he could still hear the faint, ever-present rumble from the stamp mills above town.

Jack mentally prepared for the coming Faro game. Envisioning the layout of the cards on the table, he rehearsed the view from different angles, depending on where he happened to sit, so he would be comfortable no matter which angle it took. He knew how much money he would bring to the table: no more than he could afford to lose in any one evening. Above all, he maintained a calm, semidetached attitude on the outside. In his head, he would be watching the other players for signs of weakness or overconfidence, which signaled the confidence of their next bet. Luck was a helpful companion, but having the proper frame of mind could make all the difference, no matter what the game was called.

He had become very adept at appearing to take a sip of his drink at the expected intervals during the night, but almost never feeling the effects. Unfortunately for his fellow players—and fortunately for Jack—they usually did not possess the same self-control. This often resulted in the odds favoring a less-than-inebriated young Irishman, who always departed the game while he was ahead.

He played by his own rules: honesty and sobriety, which often left his pockets bulging. But nearly as often, his departure brought the animus of inebriated players as he made his way home.

Leaving Broadway behind him, Jack walked through streets and alleys downhill into the Chinatown section until he came to a saloon called Rosemary's, a typical shotgun-style building, long and thin. Like many buildings in Granite, the front was at street level, and the back end was supported by heavy posts as the ground dropped away. The saloon's name on the wide front glass window was garishly painted in red with gold outlines. It had traditional swinging double doors—the winter doors were folded back out of sight—and a long, well-worn bar and brass rail along one wall, with several round tables opposite.

The establishment was occupied by working-class men in various stages of relieving the aches and pains of a hard day spent underground. Cigar and pipe smoke filled the air, masking the less pleasant odors of stale beer and the gaseous byproducts of pickled eggs, typical bar food of the day.

A Chinese fellow wearing a Mandarin hat was seated at a piano near the front window, playing loudly, though reasonably well. He was smiling and singing to his own accompaniment, but even though the tune was a popular and recognizable song, the words were anyone's guess.

At the back of the room was a long table laid out with the familiar green felt and accouterments of the game of Faro. Three saloon employees were ready to work the table as dealer, casekeeper, and lookout, the typical workstations of Faro. The dealer, obviously, shuffled and dealt the cards. The casekeeper operated the case, which was an abacus-like rack with spindles and beads showing how many cards in each suit were left in the deck. That way, players could strategize their bets. The lookout was mainly an overseer who ensured a fair and honest game. All were men of long-standing reputation in this establishment, and Jack looked forward to fattening his bank account this night.

Tim Kearney shouted above the piano and waved at Jack to come sit at the table beside him. Jack paused at the bar long enough to pick up a beer. While the barman was pouring, Jack nodded toward the piano player and asked, "What's he singing?"

"Why, don't you recognize 'Arkansas Traveler?'" the barman laughed. "That's Kee. We call him China Keys. He speaks good English, okay, but when he gets really wound up singin', nobody can understand him!"

Jack just smiled and paid the man, then made his way to the Faro table. For the first time in many months, his financial future was taking shape. His wages at the mine were fine enough to live on—and then some. But he knew cards could help him accumulate larger sums. He was thinking long-term now. He viewed the small games with his friends as practice, and because they were friends, he didn't try to take too much of their money. Luck is a fine thing. Skill is another. Put together, they make dreams come true.

"Evenin' Jack, my boy," said Kearney. "You know Clancy here," who nodded at Jack over his own glass.

Tim pointed to the end of the table, "These fellows are from the carpenter's shop up on the hill. And this here is Mister Wallace, and this is Mister Brown, recently arrived from Wyoming Territory. Oh, I beg your pardon, the State of Wyoming. I have yet to get used to the change of status, gentlemen, no offense."

The two strangers Kearney had told him about sat across from him and Clancy at the table. Wallace's attire was clean and formal: a well-made dark pinstripe suit and vest coat with a cleanly starched shirt and collar boards. He wore a low derby hat of expensive construction and a ring with a red stone that appeared valuable. He was of average build and smartly groomed, with a thin mustache. The overall appearance reminded Jack of professional gamblers he had seen in crooked gaming houses, where the hapless card player was relieved of his money in short order.

Brown, on the other hand, looked less comfortable, as if he wore his clothes as a costume in a play. Beneath a brown bowler, he wore a suit to match, but it was cut for a smaller man. Perhaps he had the suit made before he gained weight, or the suit was made for someone else he crossed paths with. Brown was certainly heavier than Wallace, but muscular. A few weeks' worth of stubble awaited an acquaintance with a barber. His hair below the bowler was oily, and he had a dark countenance about him, constantly shifting a wooden toothpick from one side of his mouth to the other.

In short, Jack did not wish to make a lifelong friendship with either man. He carefully half-waved his foaming beer glass at the men on the other side of the table.

Wallace lifted his own glass slightly. "None taken, sir. I can assure you it comes as a welcome change to ourselves indeed."

Wallace seemed friendly enough to Jack, but there was no smile on his lips as he spoke, and he only lightly sipped at his beer. *He may be guarding his own alcoholic limits just as I am.* Jack made a note to bid very carefully. Brown, on the other hand, made no attempt to be social and had a scowl on his face that seemed its natural expression. He neither spoke nor smiled. It was also not lost on Jack that he had no glass of beer—or any other drink in front of him.

Kearney leaned into Jack and chuckled. "I want you right next to me, Jack boy, so you know I'm not cheating."

Jack nodded toward a priest, seated at the bar with a glass in hand. "Tim, if you cheated me or anyone else, Father Michael would have you sayin' 'Our Fathers' until next Tuesday." Jack nodded toward Father Michael, who was seated at the bar, glass in hand, nodding to the beat of the music.

"Aye. The good Father takes his tea in a glass, doesn't he?" Raising his voice, Tim called, "How's your tea, Father?"

Father Michael only noticed Tim at the mention of his name, and put a hand to his ear, leaning forward, "How's that again, Timothy?"

"I say, nice to see ya, Father," shouted Kearney, laughing again.

Michael raised his glass only slightly, but seemed not to want to draw attention to his "tea."

"Okay, boys," said Tim. "Let us get to bucking the tiger and see who has the most money in his pockets. Banker, do your job."

Unlike poker, Faro was a game of chance where players bet on the likelihood of a card being drawn by the dealer. Players placed bets on the images of cards painted on the table, and the dealer adjusted the position of the box containing a shuffled deck of cards. As the bets were called, he drew the banker's card and placed it on the painted card on the table. Bets that were placed on that card lost. Then a player's card was drawn and placed on the table—bets placed on that card won.

Jack was an experienced Faro player, and Tim and Clancy were as well. The men from the mine carpenters' shop were somewhat less so and asked about rules now and then. The two strangers, Wallace and Brown, however, were unknown quantities.

The night wore on, and money came and went. The casekeeper made steady clickety noises as he arranged the counters showing which cards had been played. Unlike many Faro tables Jack had played in other towns, he knew Rosemary's ran a respectable house. There was little opportunity for a player to interfere with the odds, and in those places of low reputation where stacked card decks, or shaved or textured cards, favored the bank, Jack had learned early how to spot a poor game.

In one skinning den before leaving New York, Jack had been the rube and had lost a week's wages in less than two hours. Since that time, he carefully bided his time in new surroundings, and he now felt comfortable in Rosemary's among friends. The pianist struck up a lively rendition of "Kentucky Babe," and it seemed the room was filled to bursting with thirsty men. Conversation at the card table was held at a shout, and only the most concentrated minds could focus on the running game.

Straining to be heard didn't stop them from enjoying the boisterous company of their friends, and Jack steered the conversation here and there, hoping that either Brown or Wallace, or better yet, both, would lose track of their bets and lose more than they won. Not that their losing would benefit Jack directly in the slightest, but a heavy bank meant more money was available for a winning man.

"So, brother Tim," yelled Jack, "you never have told me why this place is named 'Rosemary's.' I've not seen the slightest hint of a woman in here, except for a sporting lady now and then."

"Ah, 'tis a sad tale indeed." Kearney pointed his cigar toward a large man wearing a barkeep's apron at the far end of the bar. "McGinty over there owns the place. He worked up at the mine until he broke his back about nine years ago. When he got on his feet again, he opened this place and named it for his wife. But the black diphtheria took her in '84, only a few months after he opened. He's been a loner ever since, but he kept the name."

Clancy finished off a glass of beer and burped. "Aye, Jack. Be glad you were not here for that plague. Thirty-five children and a lot of their parents are all down in the Philipsburg Cemetery today thanks to that black death, bless their souls."

The man named Wallace seemed to Jack the smarter— or at least more talkative—of the pair of strangers. He had roving eyes like a rodent that took in everything going on around him. He watched how each man made his bets and made his jokes, and drank his beer. And as the game wore on, it appeared the strangers would not be making many friends tonight. When they won, they hardly reacted, and when they lost, their demeanor turned even darker. The gods of Faro did not seem to favor them this night, which soured their mood even more.

The more Jack's friends drank, of course, the more rambunctious they became. Sometimes, strangers do not take well to people who make themselves too familiar too quickly.

As midnight drew near, Jack had a week's worth of room rent warming his pockets. He stood and drained his beer glass.

"Well, gents, I've had a fine evening, but my mother always taught me to respect the clock." He stretched his back. "Especially when I have a shift tomorrow."

"One more hand!" Kearney slurred.

"Let me win some rent money from you," Clancy said.

But Jack was firm and shrugged into his coat.

"Sorry, lads. This will keep me from sleeping in the churchyard next week. I must bid you good night. Mister Wallace, Mister Brown, thank you for a fine game, and I wish you good luck in the remainder. Please try not to leave these boys penniless, as I've no room for them at my place tonight."

He tipped his cap to them and made his way toward the door. On his way out, he tipped the Chinese piano player, who nodded thanks to the beat of his music, and shouted, "Thank you!"

The music and singing of the saloon had not diminished as the night matured and had, in fact, grown quite loud.

Consequently, Jack did not hear or notice the two men, Wallace and Brown, also making their excuses and bidding good night to the men at the Faro table as Jack made his way to the door. The general crowd at the bar and the banging piano drowned out the voices of Jack's friends making similar appeals for them to stay. Despite the throng, both men managed to exit the front of the saloon only a minute or two after Jack.

8

THE NIGHT WAS NOT QUITE FREEZING, BUT AT AN altitude of sixty-five hundred feet, any night was cold once the sun sank over the mountains. Jack could see the fog of his breath as he made his way up the dark street toward Broadway. No one else was about, and the even more wood smoke drifted above the rooftops. Down a side alley behind him, a dog barked slowly, as if he was unsure who was lurking.

Probably a cat wandered into the wrong yard, thought Jack.

Whenever he was alone with his thoughts, he dreamed of his saloon. *His* saloon. *That had a nice ring to it.* The fact that he had no training or education in finances or how to run a business bothered him not at all. If the beer was cold and the house was honest, Jack was sure of success.

He could see in his mind's eye the layout of the bar itself and how the gambling tables would be arrayed across the back of the room. He would live upstairs and have several rooms to let, on the far side, of course, to keep the noise away from his own living space. There would be a decent kitchen in back, too. The more services he could offer, the longer his clientele would keep playing. Whiskey, beer, and food would only be a sideline—gambling is where the real money came in.

If he could find a bartender willing to work for a little lower wages, coupled with part of the take, that would reduce some overhead. He would try to do the same for a cook. Jack never cared for the saloons that ran as a dance hall or had stage acts. He felt a stage didn't add enough income to make it worth the expense. But a piano was a must. He liked that Chinese piano player at Rosemary's just now. That would be a fine addition. And the piano player would do well on tips and a bit of wages, too. His employees would be more than just an expense. They would be like partners and feel invested in making the place great.

With many more games like he played tonight, Jack was confident in his path to riches.

He climbed the hill to the upper roadway and was thankful for the exertion. Had he not been so guarded with his drink, he might have had a warmer gut to see himself home against the chill, but he reminded himself of his promise to be fit for work tomorrow and was glad he had his senses. Even the ones that made him shiver.

It was at that moment that he glanced back in time to see a weighted leather pouch flying toward his head.

He started to twist out of the way, but too late. The sap made contact with Jack's skull. He stumbled and saw stars. A follow-up blow by his attacker sent Jack to the ground. He tried to roll out of the way, but was kicked in the side and then the stomach. Jack gasped for breath.

Wallace leaned down closely to look him in the face. "You have a sizable amount of our money," he said quietly.

His beer-and-garlic breath landed full in Jack's face. "I think you had better hand it over."

Jack wheezed. "It is not *your* money. You lost it fair and square. Then it was the bank's money and I won it fair and—"

Another kick from Brown drove the remaining air out of Jack's lungs.

Brown rifled through Jack's pockets and ripped out his money. Jack kicked out at him. Their legs became entangled, and they rolled across the alley into some bushes.

Jack landed a few blows into Brown's head and sides, but Brown was simply larger and stronger. His fists rained down on Jack from every direction. He got back to his feet and kicked Jack mercilessly.

Jack heard more than one of his ribs crack. The last few kicks went to his head. In the blackness that followed, the blows fell like thunder, drifting slowly down the mountain to the valley below.

Then he felt nothing.

$$9$$

EARLY THE FOLLOWING MORNING, A YOUNG MAN named Han Liu pushed his squeaky wooden hand cart up the alley from the Chinese laundry house, past the bottling works toward Broadway. Han was born in Granite and worked in his parents' laundry, an important part of the business community whose patrons included everyone from miners to bankers. So important, in fact, that he had tried for some time to convince his father to open a second laundry down the mountain in Philipsburg. The family had cousins in the town who were struggling with a small laundry of their own, but with the help of Han's family, he was sure they could build it into a more successful enterprise. When this morning's pickups were completed, Han and his father planned to visit with their cousins and propose a partnership. He was eager to complete his rounds so they could begin a new venture.

Han shared a room with three brothers and, being the oldest, had greater responsibilities in the family business, meaning he had more work to do.

Ten-year-old Jian was charged with maintaining the fires beneath the boiling pots of laundry in the open-air working area behind the family's house. A flat wooden platform covered by a roof with open sides allowed the laundry to continue operating throughout the year. In winter, canvas sides kept the laundry from freezing while it dried.

The middle son, Rong, who believed himself to be very close to manhood at twelve, ensured the efficient separation of clothes for the pots. He packaged clean clothes in butcher's paper and tied them with twine, ready to be returned to the customers.

Because he spoke more English than his parents, Han was responsible for most of the interaction with the paying public. He would push his cart up the hills and alleys to pick up the sheets and laundry from two of the hotels under contract in town, plus the Granite hospital twice a week, collecting his load at the break of dawn. On a normal day, he could return a full load of clean linens by sundown, which kept Dr. Brandt from scolding him if the laundry was late.

On this cool June morning, Han Liu pushed his cart up the alley and got up enough speed to top the hill onto Broadway with one attempt. When he finally got to the street, he stopped in his tracks. A groan drifted from the ditch across the road.

Partway down the embankment, just off the street was a man lying very still. At first, Han thought he might be dead, but then he coughed and groaned again. His coat was pulled over his back, and his legs were tangled and pointing uphill. There was blood on the back of the man's head, and Han feared the worst.

Han chocked the wheel of his cart with a rock and crawled down the embankment. He stopped and gathered his nerve, and bent down to see if the man was breathing. It was a white man, and that made Han even more afraid. If someone came by right now, he might be accused of being a robber, and he would have a hard time explaining the scene that presented itself.

As though worrying made it come true, Han heard the clop-clop of a horse's hooves, and a heavy wagon came into view.

Max Grindle pulled up on his reins as soon as he saw Han's cart. Max, a teamster, was making deliveries of fruit and sundries to some of the shops in town and preferred early mornings so he had the road to himself, since Nookin had become skittish around other traffic in her old age.

"Now who left this danged cart in the road?" he muttered. "How's a fellow supposed to get by?"

He looked around, then down into the ditch, where he was startled to see Han hovering over a prostrate body. Max knew a robbery when he saw one. He pulled an old Colt Navy revolver from under his coat and pointed it at Han.

"Hey—Get away from that man! Git your hands up and get up here!"

Max climbed down from the wagon as Han crawled up from the ditch, alternately putting his hands up over his head and his palms together in front of him, in his panic, pleading in Cantonese for the teamster not to shoot him.

"Mh hóu hōi chèung!" Completely forgetting to even try to say "don't shoot" in English.

"Ho-hi nothin'. You stand still, boy."

Max sidestepped down the embankment, keeping his gun pointed at Han. He reached down with his free hand to roll the unconscious man onto his back.

As soon as Max pulled on his shoulder, Jack yelped in pain, and Max stopped.

"Take it easy, mister. You look like a mile of bad track."

It was obvious to Max by then that Han had nothing to do with the wounded man's condition. It was much worse than it looked from up on the street, and this skinny kid probably couldn't muster one good punch if he had to.

Max holstered his pistol and motioned for Han to help him drag the moaning, bloodied man up the hill and lift him into his wagon. Between the two of them, they managed to lay Jack flat on his back. Jack was wheezing and couldn't catch his breath. The swelling of his face was such that he could barely open one eye.

Max drove off toward the hospital, with Han slowly following, pushing his laundry cart. Han was grateful that Max had come upon the scene, despite nearly getting shot, as he could hardly have managed to drag Jack up the hillside and lift him into his cart. He was also hopeful that Doctor Brandt would overlook him being late to pick up the day's laundry. It then dawned on Han that his planned trip with his father down to Philipsburg would have to wait. He would simply have to explain the events and convince him to see the cousins tomorrow.

Lying in the back of the wagon, drifting in and out of consciousness, Jack tried to remember how he got there and why he was hurting so badly, but it just wouldn't come to him. He bounced along on the rough boards, grunting in pain at each thump of the wagon wheels as they rolled over even small rocks and ruts in the street. He passed out again and was still unconscious when they reached the hospital.

Max reined his team up to the receiving doors and ran inside to fetch someone to help him. No one was there at such an early hour, and he had to search the halls of the first floor before he bumped into Jillian Brandt coming out of one of the open wards with an armload of linens.

"Miss Jillian, there's a man out in my wagon who's near death from a bad beatin'. Can you come help me get him inside?"

She dropped the linens on a bench. "Show me."

She followed Max to the wagon. Jack was half awake but moaning and gagging again, trying to get a full breath.

Jillian called to Wallace Coates, who had heard the commotion and came running down the hall, to bring a stretcher down the cement ramp at the receiving entrance. They all carried Jack inside and laid the stretcher on a table in the examining room. Coates ran to find Dr. Brandt.

Jillian leaned over and looked at Jack's swollen face. His left eye was shut tight from swelling on that side of his face, and the right was only a small slit. It looked like he was trying to focus.

Jack, slightly conscious again, imagined an angel hovering above him. He believed he had truly expired and was being welcomed into heaven by the most beautiful face he had ever seen. His first reaction was to smile, but then the world turned black yet again.

"I think he's awake," said Jillian, and then an instant later, "Oh… No, he's not."

She pointed to a big water pitcher on the counter and gathered a washcloth and bandages from a nearby cabinet.

"Max, set some of that water to boil. We'll need some hot water to clean these cuts."

Dr. Brandt walked in briskly and went immediately to Jack's side to assess his wounds. "Well, well. Isn't this a different way to begin the day?"

The obvious cuts and swelling to Jack's face were the least important injuries at the moment. Whatever was preventing him from breathing properly took priority. Brandt felt down each of Jack's sides, top to bottom, and then back up, and stepped back. "Well, he has at least two broken ribs. No telling how many more are bruised and almost broken."

"His right eye seems to focus," said Jillian, "but with all that swelling, he hasn't opened the left one yet."

She brought the pot of water to the tray beside the exam table and laid out clean cloths and bandages. Brandt sent the orderly out to the ice house behind the building for cold water and some ice to help with the swelling. Then he began cutting Jack's shirt off to allow access to his chest and ribs.

"Who is he? Does anyone know his name?" asked Jillian.

"He was in a ditch up the street from Rosemary's," Max said. "At first I thought that Chinese kid was about to rob him, but I guess he was tryin' to help. This fella looks like he was a-layin out there all night."

Han Liu slipped into the room and watched quietly from the corner.

Jillian frowned, "Han wouldn't rob a fly. He's our laundry man, and he has enough work to do without getting into trouble and running from the law."

"Yes, ma'am," said Max. "This guy sure took a beatin'."

She turned to Han and pointed out in the hallway. "Han, you can start with the pile I dropped in the hall. The rest is in the kitchen."

Han bowed slightly. "Yes, Ma'am," and moved on about his business.

Jillian washed the cuts on Jack's face, and they wrapped his ribcage tightly. Dr. Brandt and the orderly moved Jack into a room on the main floor where he could be more easily monitored. No patients were residing in the upstairs rooms, and with these injuries, Brandt thought the young man might not last more than a day or two. So why bother carrying him upstairs only to have to carry him back down again so soon? He had seen his share of battered men from bar fights and mining accidents, and this one had little chance of surviving if his breathing didn't improve. Brandt was sure he had a concussion to boot.

If his brain didn't swell too much, he might avoid the risk of trephination and its attendant complications. Doctor Brandt had performed the operation more than once. Sometimes treating battle wounds, sometimes for a simple kick to a trooper's head from a high-spirited cavalry horse.

He personally had a fifty percent success rate. Of those patients on whom he had removed a circular portion of cranial bone, half had survived the initial procedure. Of those, about half died of subsequent infection or other complications. With such a high mortality rate, it was only done as a last resort.

Hours later, Jack opened his eyes but could only see a little out of his right eye, enough to know he was in a hospital room. When he tried turning his head, it caused lightning bolts to stab through his skull. He was covered with a sheet, and he could tell he was missing some of his clothes. He could not move any of his appendages without pain. When he tried to sit up, his ribs ground together, his vision blurred, and he passed out again.

Jillian and the orderly took turns checking on Jack's ragged, wheezing breathing throughout the day. Around dinner time, she brought a bowl of cool water and a cloth to wipe Jack's brow and face.

She leaned over the bed and softly asked, "Are you awake?"

He grunted in response.

"I'm sorry you're in such pain, sir. We've done our best for you, but you need to rest. Maybe tomorrow you'll tell us your name."

Jack's eye finally focused on her, and she smiled.

To Jack, it was as if the sun had just come out after a storm. The thunder was still echoing in his head, though, and when he tried to speak, it was just a gurgle.

"Shhhh. You rest." Jillian quietly left the room. Jack took a breath and was rewarded with new pain. He decided to follow the angel's orders and closed his eye.

10

THE SUN WAS STILL BEHIND THE MOUNTAIN WHEN
the steam whistle on the hoist house at the Ruby Shaft blew its long lament, signaling the beginning of another shift. Men carrying lunch pails trudged up the hill and waited their turn to board the cage that would carry them down into the bowels of the earth. As each man inched toward the shaft gate, he dug in his pocket and hung his numbered metal tag on a wooden board, "tagging in," to signify that he was underground in the event of an accident.

The shift boss, Brownlow, waved at Tim Kearney to get his attention over the noise of the hoist and the rock drills below.

Kearney inched forward with the line but was not about to give up his place, waiting instead for Brownlow to come to him. The sooner he got down the shaft, he felt, the sooner he could return. The shift was eight hours long, but time moved faster when you weren't standing around waiting in line. Kearney worked all his life in the mines, but didn't particularly like being underground. Braving the depths was a means to an end. The wages he earned a thousand feet away from the light of day were meant to provide a life for him and his wife, if he lived long enough to find one.

Brownlow leaned close. "Where's Fallon?"

Kearney looked back at the line of men and shrugged. "Haven't seen him yet this morning, boss."

"I'll dock him half a day if he's late by a minute! We don't tend shirkers in my gang, Kearney."

"I'm sure he'll be along, don't you worry. He's a hard workin' boy, our Jack."

Brownlow shifted his cigar from one side of his mouth to the other and stalked out of the hoist house.

Kearney leaned back to the redhead behind him. "Boy-o, that Jack better fly like a bird if he wants to keep his job, eh, Clancy?"

But no bird named Jack alighted in the mine cage that morning, and by suppertime, Kearney began to worry whether he had come down with a serious case.

Halfway through the shift, Brownlow was forced to tell the mine manager, Tom Kelley, about the absence of one of his gang.

Kelley didn't suffer shirkers either. He considered himself a good judge of character, and Fallon hadn't struck him as the type to disappear before payday. Kelley surmised that if nothing else, Fallon would at least show up for his wages two days hence. And if he didn't show up soon, they'd be his last.

He sent McFeeney to make some inquiries around town. Grabbing his bowler hat off the hat tree by the door, he thought of places to look.

"And don't forget to check the calaboose!" Kelley called after him.

The town jail, or calaboose, was a simple one-room building used as a holding cell down the hill near Chinatown. It mostly held rowdy drunks until they were sane and sober again. Serious crimes brought the sheriff up from Philipsburg, where a real jail awaited.

Even if Kelley hadn't told him to check the jail, McFeeney would have started there. He hadn't been in the card game the night before, but he was one of the boisterous singers at Rosemary's and saw that Jack had left the card game around midnight. But who knew if he might have stopped off for another nip on the way to his room.

McFeeney went down Broadway and cut through the alley beside the Windsor House boarding rooms, around the corner of the bottling works, then downhill behind a handful of smaller buildings occupied by the Chinese. To him, it was only natural that the jail be located in such a low neighborhood.

The jail was a twelve-foot square one-room log structure with only one small window in a heavy wood and iron door. The calaboose was generally thought of as simply a safe place to put a man who might injure himself while ranting on matters of great importance and logic, understandable only to himself in his inebriated state. The low roof and the only light from the small window in the door resembled the worst part of mining: the underground darkness. It served as hard rehabilitation of the unfortunate occupant. A day or two spent in such confinement was reason enough to limit one's intake of whiskey, or so its builders hoped. The cure usually lasted at least until payday.

When first erected, the jail had only a heavy wooden beam placed across iron brackets to secure the prisoner inside, but too many men had found early freedom through the aid of well-meaning though equally intoxicated friends, so a large padlock was added to ensure the prisoner had sobered sufficiently before being released. The keys were held by responsible citizens of the town: the manager of the Granite Mountain Mining Company, the president of Granite Miners' Union, and the town doctor.

McFeeney could smell the place before he got close. No one was responsible for keeping it clean, so it never lost the stench of vomit, urine, and excrement. All lent even more encouragement to the rehabilitation process.

McFeeney took a deep breath and walked closer to the small window. "Hey, Jack! Jack Fallon, are you in there?"

Expending his one good breath, he stepped back to take another and heard a moan from within, followed by a cough as someone awoke inside the dark jail.

"Who's there? McFeeney? Is that you?" A man coughed and spat. McFeeney heard him struggle to his feet. "Run and fetch us a bottle, there's a good man."

"Who's that?" McFeeney asked.

"Dammit, Mac! It's your old pal Pat Durnigan." He coughed long and phlegmy again, louder this time, and spat. "I'm sorry, old son, I don't mean to be cross. Forget about a bottle. Go find a key and get me out 'a here, like a good lad. I'll miss my shift, I will."

"Sure, Pat," said McFeeney. He couldn't see in the window and wasn't about to venture any closer to the stinking jail cell than he had to. "Say, I don't suppose you've seen Jack Fallon?"

"Who?"

"Never mind. I'll send someone to open the door, Pat. Soon as I can."

As he left, Durnigan's cries and cursing for immediate relief receded with the stink of the jail. He headed back up to Main Street, intending to check some of the saloons along the way to the Union Hall. Just then, Jigger Smith, a man from third shift, came up the hill from the town hospital.

Smith waved with his bandaged arm. "Hey, Mac! I'm off for two days. Want to join me at the Union Hall for a pint? Had a disagreement with the four-foot saw in the carpenter's shop, so I spent a relaxing morning in the company of that nurse. Twenty-two stitches."

McFeeney didn't break stride and kept walking past Jigger down the hill. "I can't. I'm on the hunt for a guy missing from first shift."

Jigger turned as he passed, "Didja check the tags?"

"No, he's not missing down the hole, you dumb cluck. He missed his shift entirely."

"I heard there's a guy up the hospital who hasn't woke up from a bender last night," Jigger called, continuing on course for the Union Hall and a cold beer.

That caught McFeeney's attention, and he changed course. He waved at Jigger and turned toward the hospital.

McFeeney didn't like hospitals in general, nor doctors in particular. He had never had need of either one, which was unusual for a man employed around the mines. But it was his firmly held belief that doctors were all drunkards, and that when a man's time came to die, he had better do it without procrastination brought on by modern medicine, the quicker for his lads to set about their wake over his remains.

Arriving at the doors to the Granite Hospital, McFeeney set his jaw and stepped up to the porch and went in. The odor of septic cleansers and mysterious medical smells solidified his trepidation at entering death's playground. He hoped to find the doctor quickly and learn if Fallon was indeed on the registry, but instead, he was met just inside the entryway by the doctor's stunning young wife. He had seen her before from a distance, but this was the closest he'd ever been, and knew at once who she was.

McFeeney swiped the hat off his balding head. "I'm sorry, ma'am, but I'm looking for a fellow who didn't show for his work today. Jack Fallon. Would you by chance know if he's one of your charges hereabouts?"

"Well, we do have a gentleman patient, but he's not been able to speak as yet. It would be a great help to us if you could look in on him and tell me if he is the man you named."

McFeeney was loath to venture any further into this sad realm. On the other hand, if this beautiful creature had asked, he would have ventured into the gates of hell. "Why, sure, I'd follow you anywh— that is to say, yes, ma'am." He cleared his throat. "I can take a look if you wish."

Jillian led the way down the hall to Jack's room. As they stepped through the open door, McFeeney looked at Jack's swollen countenance and whistled softly. He had seen men bloodied and beaten before, but Jack's condition still took his breath away.

He cocked his head to one side as if to line up his sight with the swollen, bruised face on the pillow, nodded once, and finally said, "Yes, miss. I mean, ma'am. That's our Jack. What's happened to him?"

"Sorry to say, we have no idea. He was brought in nearly as you see him. He has some broken ribs and a bad concussion, and the rest, you can see, is quite serious. You say he works at the mine?"

"Well, yes, ma'am. Who don't? I mean to say, he'll be fired if he misses his shift."

Doctor Brandt walked in. "He'll not be working any shifts for the foreseeable future, McFeeney. Can't you see he's dancing with death already?"

"Sorry, Doctor. I'll let the yard boss know. And thank you. Thank you, too, ma'am."

He made a quick departure, thankful to be out of that place, and at the same time, understanding the effect Mrs. Brandt's presence had on his friends who had been to the hospital. In the hard life of a miner, real beauty made a memorable impression. With a sigh, he headed back to Kelley's office to answer the mystery.

$$11$$

LATER THAT MORNING, DR. BRANDT BENT OVER Jack, who had beads of sweat on his forehead. Although the swelling on his face was unchanged, he seemed flushed. Brandt surmised he had developed a fever, either from an infection or from lying unconscious in a cold ditch all night.

He told Jillian to administer hourly wetting baths to try to bring the fever down. He knew she would properly assign the task to an orderly. He also asked her to try to get some broth or soup into him to keep his strength up.

Jillian acknowledged his orders and went to record Jack's name in the hospital record. At the admitting desk, she drew a line through the original entry of "Unknown" next to Jack's initial admission date and wrote in his name. Now that they knew he was a miner, it would help them obtain payment from the company. The hospital was built and owned by the Granite Mining Company for the benefit of the miners and employees, which included almost all of the town's residents. When a miner came in for treatment, he need only provide his name and tag to be treated, and the bill would be paid by the Company. Town residents who weren't in the mine's employ paid their own expenses. Indigents with no money to pay usually received less care and attention. Just enough to get them out of the hospital and save expenses.

Dr. Brandt still held no high hopes for Jack's recovery, but since the company was paying the medical bills, he was willing to provide all the treatment a patient could need. He no longer held expectations for miracles. Men lived and died, and that was that. His doctoring often made little difference, as the worst wounds of mining—like the wounds of battle he had seen in the Army—were not usually survivable. A quick recovery was preferable, however, as there was an inkling in the back of his mind that Jillian had an odd look about her when she was in the room with Jack.

Jillian, on the other hand, had the greatest hope for Jack to return to health. She still possessed the untarnished innocence of a woman unjaded by life's cruelties. In her mind's eye, she saw the beauty in things others ignored. This young miner, even though he had yet to speak, lacked the rough exterior to which she had grown accustomed. Married though she was, she noticed he was handsome—or would be, once his wounds healed.

Even the tension—she was yet unwilling to call it unhappiness—of her marriage did not tarnish her belief in better things for those who deserved them. She believed she could have done worse. There had been few prospects when she was younger—only miners, mostly—and they were a gruff type, with shallow thoughts and briefer needs.

Alone in his room, Jack's body slowly began the long journey back to health. Time spent in pain has its own clock, and sleep is the hour hand. In his bed, Jack took stock of his wounds as his head cleared a little at a time. He still could not draw a deep breath without stabbing pain. He could see well enough out of his right eye, but the left was only now beginning to admit light through a slender crack. He raised his hands, bringing fresh pain from his chest, and he saw that his knuckles were bloodied and swollen.

At least I got some licks in. Though he could remember almost nothing about the battle that brought him here.

He tried to relax. He wished desperately to cough, as his chest was tight with fluid, but each attempt hurt so badly, he barely managed to clear his throat. The pounding in his head felt like the rhythmic hoisting machinery at the mine.

"The mine!" he whispered. "I've missed my shift! I'll be fired if I don't—"

He started to push himself up on his elbows, but the room swam, and he was again enveloped in darkness.

Later, he awoke as he was being propped up on pillows by Jillian.

"Thank you," he said through puffy lips and a thick tongue, sounding more like, "Fang-u."

Jillian raised an eyebrow with a smile. "So. You still have your manners, Mr. Fallon. You've been a worry, you certainly have."

She reached for a bowl of soup on the nightstand beside the bed and laid a napkin on Jack's chest.

"How long…"

"Well, you came to us very early this morning. You're in the Granite Hospital, and Doctor Brandt says you have broken ribs and a concussion."

She spooned a little soup into his mouth. He closed his eyes and tried to swallow.

"You can feel your injuries, so you don't need me to tell you to be careful and take it easy until you're well."

"But I have to get to my shift. I'll lose my job," he said, his voice still muffled.

Jillian was used to men overestimating themselves when it came to grave injuries. *They all think they're Hercules.*

"You don't know how badly you're hurt. You would barely make it out of the building, let alone up to the mine. So just accept the fact that you're laid up, and concentrate on rest and recuperation."

"But—" Jack lifted his sheets and discovered his clothes were missing. "My God! Where are my clothes?"

"In order to care for you, we have to keep your wounds clean."

She left the rest unsaid, and color rose in Jack's cheeks as he let his head fall back on the pillow.

Jillian suppressed an unprofessional giggle and reminded herself of her position. As a nurse and, more importantly, a married woman. It was the hospital orderlies, of course, who were responsible for Jack's general hygiene and bathing while he lay unconscious. But if embarrassment kept him in a cooperative mood, then so be it.

This man is no different from any other patient, and the sooner he accepts me as the one in control of his situation, the better.

"As I said, you're not going anywhere."

Jack did not really feel like working, but his sense of responsibility urged him to find a way to try to keep his employment.

Sensing his thoughts, Jillian said, "You needn't worry about your job at the mine. A man came looking for you and told us you're an employee of the company. Dr. Brandt will do whatever is needed for you to return to work, and for as long as that takes."

With that, she delivered more soup into Jack's mouth, which had opened in protest, thus ending the argument.

12

"WHAT DO YOU MEAN HE'S NEAR DEATH?" ASKED Tom Kelley.

"Jack's layin' up in the hospital all beat so bad he can't talk or wake up," said McFeeney. "I tell ya, boss, he looks like he tried to chop down a tree with his face. They said someone found him like that this morning in Chinatown. Said his pockets and clothes were all ripped. I guess he was robbed. Some of the fellows had a big card game down there the night before."

"Damn. Get Brownlow to find one of Fallon's shift mates and bring him here. I'll see if he knows what happened. I might need the sheriff from down in town, so after you tell Brownlow, find a horse and come back here."

McFeeney raced out to find the shift boss, Brownlow.

It would take a while for his instructions to be carried out, so Kelley grabbed his hat and went to inform Superintendent Weir what had happened. He hoped Weir's influence might encourage the sheriff to take speedy action and hunt down the robber, if that is indeed what occurred. He wouldn't know until all the facts were gathered.

Hundreds of feet below ground, Tim Kearney grimaced, finishing a ladle of rancid water from the water wagon. It wasn't quite time to think about lunch, but a bite from his pail would take the foul taste out of his mouth. As he walked back to the last crosscut in the tunnel to grab a nip of pasty from his lunch, he was met by an Italian fellow he knew only in passing, Giolo-something.

"You Kearney?" he asked.

Tim nodded.

"Brownlow wants you up top. He says come right now."

What was this? Calling a guy off the drift never happened. Maybe if his wife had a baby, but that certainly didn't apply to Kearney. He hurried to the shaft and rang the proper sequence of bells to call the lift. All the while, he couldn't help but think of Jack's absence that morning.

By the time he got to the mine office, Tom Kelley was just returning from telling Weir what little he knew.

"What's happened? Is it Jack?" he shouted as he ran up.

"He's down in the hospital." He had to grab Kearney to stop him from continuing on to the hospital. "Now wait, tell me about the card game last night."

"What? Just me and the boys. Jack won pretty good, but he left around midnight. What happened to him?"

"It sounds like he was robbed and beat up pretty bad."

"Those two strangers! Brown and Wallace. Couple of out-of-towners. Riverboat gamblers, I'd say. They left right after Jack."

"Okay. We'll bring the sheriff up from town. You go see if Jack can speak yet. Wait—First, go visit The Dry. You're covered in mud."

The mine superintendent, Weir, had implemented a new concept in mining work, the "dry house," where hot, sweaty miners coming off shift could change clothes and clean up before emerging into the winter cold. Incidents of pneumonia and other ailments dropped, and, of course, the company benefited from having healthy working men. He also ordered the construction of the company hospital, in which young Jack was now recovering.

Tim jogged back to the mine to clean up a bit, all the while blaming himself for letting those two card sharps in the game.

Before Kelley opened the office door, McFeeney came riding around the corner, unsteadily mounted on a quarter horse borrowed from the woodcutters' crew.

"I found a horse, Mr. Kelley!" he said, tugging on the reins, trying in vain to get the animal to stop circling.

Kelley said, "Well, put it back. Mr. Weir himself is taking his carriage down to fetch Sheriff Cole."

McFeeney looked both dejected for having lost his important job of calling in the law and relieved at not having to ride all that way. He was no horseman, and it was the limit of his skill just to get the horse this far.

It was late afternoon by the time John Cole arrived at the Granite Hospital from Philipsburg. He was met by Dr. Brandt at the receiving entrance, who took him immediately to see Jack, who was sleeping fitfully. Brandt listened to his chest and was still concerned about sounds of fluid in Jack's lungs. After a few movements of the stethoscope, Jack awoke, startled at the crowd of people in his room.

Tim Kearney stood closest by his bedside, with Brandt opposite. Around the foot of his bed, Jack saw only strangers.

"Mr. Fallon, we've not met. I am Thomas Weir, Superintendent of the Granite Mining Company."

The mine superintendent was a devout Presbyterian with strong morals and cared very much for his workers, whether on the job or, like Jack, in whatever troubles they found themselves.

Weir had an equally strong background in the mining business, arriving in Granite in 1888 by way of Nebraska and Leadville, Colorado, and was widely respected. Everyone, it seemed, liked the man who was responsible for initiating the six-day work week, when it had been a longstanding practice to work all seven, regardless of the good Lord's instruction to the contrary. Weir ensured the boarding houses at Granite were maintained, cleaned, and fumigated. His $3.50 per day wage was also above average. His concern for his men showed on his face just now.

Weir continued, "This is John Cole; he's the sheriff down in Philipsburg."

Jack nodded, and the sheriff spoke. "Mr. Fallon, I've been told you had some trouble after a card game last night."

Jack started to speak, but went into fits of weak coughing. Kearney poured him a glass of water from a pitcher on his bedside table. Jack took a few moments to get his breathing under control.

"Some trouble," he frowned. Not for the first time, he thought about the sizeable sum that had been ripped from his pockets that night. As hazy as his memory of the attack was, he fully recalled thinking on his way home that with a number of successful games like that, he'd have his saloon-building money in no time. Now he was dismayed by the blow to his finances. "That's true. Did you catch them yet?"

"'Them?' There was more than one man?"

Kearney spoke up, "Yes, sir, if it's who we think it was, there were two strangers at Rosemary's last night. Professional gamblers. They joined our game and, well, they really didn't like losing. Who does? We didn't think nothing of it at the time, but they left right after Jack here."

He and Jack then described Wallace and Brown, in sometimes colorful language, while Cole took down the particulars.

Finally, he asked Jack, "Do you remember about how much money you had?"

"I don't remember 'about' how much, I know *exactly* how much. I ended the night with two hundred and eleven dollars in my coat pockets. Eighty-seven in my left pocket that I used to bet with, and one hundred twenty-four in the right, that I won." Saying the amount out loud angered Jack all over again at his losses.

The sheriff finished his notes, and by then Jack was sleepy again, so the others went out to the hallway.

Kearney stayed with Jack. He still felt guilty over letting the strangers in the game. He whispered, "Jack-O, you should've stayed and let me win that last eighty-seven from ya."

Out in the hallway, the sheriff told Weir he would organize a few deputies and check hotels and the train station down in town, but he warned them that if the criminals had already boarded a train, there was very little chance of catching up to them. He said he would wire the stations in Drummond and Missoula with their descriptions and hope for the best.

"In my experience, men like that know how to disappear fast. I'm sure this isn't their first card game."

13

ON FRIDAY MORNING, TOM KELLEY BUTTONED HIS jacket as he walked downhill from the company office toward the Superintendent's house on Magnolia Street. An office boy had brought a message that Kelley was wanted at the Weir's office, and he immediately grabbed his derby hat and headed out the door. He hoped there was news about the sheriff's search, though he held out little hope of the thieves being brought to justice.

The hell with justice. Bring 'em back here to my boys for an hour. They'll get justice.

The well-worn path from the general office, where Kelley worked, led to the hillside behind Weir's house on Magnolia Street.

A plank walkway led from the hillside directly to his second-story private office. Weir himself was forced to climb to the second-floor entrance outside the house each morning, as there was no connection between the upstairs and downstairs inside the stately residence. No one knew if this was an oversight by the architect or an intentional means of separating business from family life.

Kelley straightened his hat and knocked lightly on the superintendent's door. Over the rumble from the stamp mills less than a half-mile up the mountainside, he heard Weir call out, "Come."

"Mr. Weir, sir. You sent for me?" Kelley removed his derby as he closed the door behind him.

Weir sat at his six-foot-long oak desk piled high with company paperwork, production reports, assay results, payroll ledgers, and all manner of things concerning the day-to-day management of a busy industrial complex.

He handed Kelley a folded newspaper. Without waiting for Kelley to gain the gist of the front page article in the two-week-old *New York Times*, Weir grumbled, "That idiot has convinced Congress to repeal the Silver Purchase Act."

The Sherman Act was passed three years earlier, partially in response to the urging by successful mining companies who had begun to see a decline in the value of silver. The Act required the federal government to buy four and a half billion dollars' worth of silver every month, a huge windfall for the mining interests who had been overproducing thanks to technological advances in mining and silver extraction processes.

But as investors exchanged silver treasury notes for gold in such quantities that the nation's gold reserves ran dangerously low, the intent of the Act was lost. When Grover Cleveland was inaugurated, he quickly convinced Congress to overturn the Silver Purchase Act. As a result, the price of silver plummeted, and many previously successful mines began to close. It became known as the Silver Crash of 1893, and it hit mines across the country.

Kelley shifted his attention from the events of yesterday. The misfortune of one miner took a secondary place compared to the interests of the company.

"Which idiot is that, sir?" Kelley was not politically astute, but even he knew Washington, at any given point in history, was rife with idiots.

"The President. Cleveland. This whole economic mess was his fault to begin with; now he's making it worse."

"Yes, sir, that sounds bad." Kelley figured it was better to agree with the boss while hoping to learn on which side his bread would fall. "But what does it mean for us?"

"I'll tell you what it means. The boys thought it was grand when they went on six-day work weeks. They'll soon look back and *wish* they could get six days' work in two weeks."

Kelley's eyebrows rose. What was Weir saying? The mines were in danger of shutting down? They had had such good times for so long in Granite, it wasn't possible, was it?

"Don't worry, Tom," Weir said. "I'll do my best to keep things on an even keel here. Just know the situation, and for God's sake, don't spread it around. There'll be hard days ahead, and I don't want men running off in a panic. If I'm right, and I truly hope I am not, there will be some hard decisions to make very soon."

Kelley swallowed hard. "Yes, sir, I see what you mean. If we have to lay men off, though…"

"I hope it won't come to that, believe me. Maybe we can shift people around, get enough hours covered to keep the machines running. I just wanted you to know what's coming. Start thinking in terms of how we can keep up production, and who might be dead weight and needs to go. I'll try and keep you abreast of things."

"Yes. Thank you. I'll do my best."

"How is that boy? The one who was robbed?" asked Weir.

"Dr. Brandt says he might pull through. It's been dicey, but he says each day he's a little better."

"A shame. Something like that happening in our town. Is he a good man?"

"Oh, yes, sir. Steady worker. And popular with the lads."

"Thank you for coming down, Thomas."

Kelley reached for the door, and Weir spoke again, "Thomas?" Kelley turned back.

"When you start making a list of who's to be let go, I don't want his name on it. Understand? That boy's had enough bad luck."

Kelley nodded vigorously. Weir turned his attention back to his desk and waved his hand in dismissal.

As Kelley pulled the door behind him, Weir called out, "And keep the other thing quiet!"

Kelley's head spun as he climbed the path back toward the company office. Thousands of people in this town alone—not to mention the towns with mines less than a day's ride from here—depended on the mines and their money for dear life. He had seen cutbacks over the years— veins come and go, strikes peter out—but he never saw one of the big bosses as worried as he had just seen Weir. He had enough time with the company to be reasonably certain that he would be among the few who could hang on until the end, but he forced himself not to think about the younger men with families who might soon be out of work.

Back in his own office, he looked around the busy room at friends who may soon hold him responsible for being laid off. Although he would have little say in the matter, he would be the messenger of any bad news. Some of them had been with him for years, some only a few months. Without taking off his hat, he signaled to McFeeney, who joined him near the door.

"I'm taking my lunch at the union hall," Kelley said.

"'Tis hardly ten in the morning, Mr. Kelley. I never knew you for a, well—"

"Shut up, McFeeney!" He continued in a near whisper, "I'll be at the Union Hall if anyone's looking for me. Wait… If anyone asks, you don't know where I am. You come and get me yourself. Understand?"

"Sure, boss."

This was one of those times when McFeeney knew better than to ask questions. He wasn't stupid; he just pretended sometimes.

Eyes and ears open and mouth shut, Mac, and you'll learn more.

Whatever was brewing, he could tell it was big.

Kelley left the office and headed down Broadway on foot, turning the whole conversation with Weir over in his mind. There were storm clouds on the horizon, and he owed Jimmy Gilfillen a fair warning that trouble was coming. His allegiance was to the company, of course, but he would need Gilfillen's help to do what Weir commanded: keep things on an even keel, hopefully long enough to weather the coming storm. Higher-ups were always fretting over what *might* happen, and usually, nothing did. One day, they could laugh at all this. But until then, he'd better get things right with the union.

Gilfillen was the president of the Granite Miners' Union, and as such, he could be trusted to keep things quiet when it benefited his membership. And he could help keep the workers under control when the days ahead grew dark. Since it was just past ten in the morning, Kelley expected that Gilfillen would be in his office, down Main Street in the three-story Granite Miner's Union Hall. Kelley—and, come to think of it, most of the residents and almost every miner in town—had spent many pleasant times in the place. *Dances, weddings, funerals—our best days and our worst days.*

Sketching out possibilities in his head, he imagined how many men per shift could be laid off and still operate, then how many shifts he could operate per week with a given number of men. All the while, the darkness loomed over town businesses suffering and closing to the point where there weren't even enough services to keep the mine open, or the men fed and housed. At that point, he refused to let himself consider what "worst days" might lie ahead.

He walked past the first two doors that opened into the main salon of the Hall, and instead entered the smaller third door that opened to a staircase near the corner of the building. He could hear the click of billiard balls in the main salon as he ascended the stairs to the third-floor offices in search of President Gilfillen.

A man whose name he couldn't recall greeted Kelley at the union office anteroom overlooking the street. Before he could ask where the president might be found, Jim Gilfillen called to him to come into his office. He was a heavy-set, muscular man who had risen from hard-rock miner to a powerful position in organized labor. The days when he used his muscle to make things happen were behind him now, and his large frame was a bit softer than it looked.

"Good morning to you, Tom. Isn't it the middle of your working day yet?"

Kelley softly closed the office door and took off his hat, pulling a chair close to Gilfillen's desk. His nervousness was contagious, and Gilfillen knew something was bothering the man.

"Never mind about the time of day, Jimmy," he said. "I've got something of importance to say, but first I need you to know I'm not supposed to mention it to anyone."

Gilfillen's brow furrowed. "What is it, Tom? One of your boys got some poor girl in the family way?" He grinned. "Again?"

"Stop it, Jimmy. Have you been reading the papers about this silver thing the government's doing?"

"Oh, that." Gilfillen leaned back in his chair as if to blow it off. "The government thinks it's in control, but you look at what the unions have proudly done for this country. This silver and gold business is always going up and down. Don't you worry. Still, I suppose we'll be tightening our belts, eh?"

"'Tightening our belts' is it? I've just come from the superintendent's office, and I tell you I've never seen him so worried. I know we've all seen some of this coming, but I think we're looking at a terrible storm."

"Weir's uneasy about the price of silver dropping, is he? Well, aren't we all? Listen, Tom, you and I have been at this a long time. Prices come up and go down, don't they? I'll tell you what—if they start laying us off—and I'm not saying we'll go without a fight—these boys can get work in other mines or change their line of work entirely. Remember when you were a young lad and didn't know what to do with your strong back? You worked in freighting, as I recall. They'll be fine. And besides, I'm here to make sure the company treats them all right, if you take my meaning."

He leaned back in his chair, drew a thin cigar from his vest pocket, and began to light it.

"Just keep them from striking, for God's sake," said Kelley. "If we're to save anything of our jobs, and hope to have jobs to come back to afterward, I'm begging you to help us get through what's coming. If I read Mr. Weir correctly, what's coming is going to push us right to the brink. To the brink."

Gilfillen pursed his lips and calmly blew a thick curl of smoke toward the ceiling. He nodded.

"Tom, I can read a newspaper as good as the next fellow. What we're talking about here is not news to any man on this mountain. If things get rough, you've no worries from me, or this union."

He stood up, extended his hand, and they shook.

"I'm glad you came over, Tom. And you're right to try and keep things quiet as long as possible. But don't be surprised if the boys are way ahead of you on that news."

Kelley said his thanks and hurried out of the office and back down the stairs. He had done his best. Now he had to wait on events that were far beyond anyone's control on Granite Mountain.

14

JACK SQUIRMED IN HIS BED AND WONDERED HOW much longer he would be held in this prison before he could get back to work and earn his wages. With nothing to do all day but sleep and eat, he was restless. The only brightness in each day was the frequent visits by Jillian Brandt. While his body mended itself, he imagined all sorts of witty conversations he might have with her, though he forgot most of them, dozing off so often.

But when he was wide awake, he resolved to get his life back on track and back to work.

He had learned early on, even before he came to America, that in mining—and probably most jobs involving heavy labor—there was no patience for slackers. He had seen men fired for any infraction, and there were always many more men waiting to take their place. A man could make his way in the world only if he worked hard. But if Jack's idea for a high-class saloon became a reality, and if he could manage to hang onto his money, his backbreaking days would be over. He'd have his own saloon and a percentage of every game played in it.

Until then, he was on his chosen path, to work until he could be his own boss.

He had learned that American mines were populated by men driven in a way Jack had never experienced in his homeland. Back there, it was only a job and nothing more. A job handed down from generation to generation, like a fine watch. Here, the lust for gold was something Jack could understand but not wrap his hands around, as he had no thirst for it. Gold was just money, and he didn't mind working for that. Mining was a job to put food in his belly and clothes on his back. Between his steady work ethic and luck at the gaming tables, he was able to earn a comfortable lifestyle. "Comfortable" to Jack meant a warm coat and clean sheets—not a fancy house and lands. Jack came from a family and a society that believed in happiness as a simple thing, and to be satisfied with little, for then you will not be disappointed.

At the end of his shift that day, Tim Kearney returned to Jack's hospital room. He was awake but impatient to be out, even though he knew he was in no condition for hard labor.

"How are ya feelin', Jack?" said Tim. "Up for some company?"

Jack's face brightened, all thoughts of Jillian and saloons forgotten. Boredom was a heavy weight, and anything that interrupted his pastime of counting the cracks in the ceiling was welcome.

"Boy, that's what I need. It's boring layin' here all day."

Tim pulled a chair closer to the bed and relaxed into it after a hard day. His hair was still wet from his quick ablutions at The Dry.

"The fellows all said you're missed, and they hope to seeya soon. Some of them said they'll stop by later, or maybe tomorrow." He knew their intentions were supportive, but visiting a hospital was difficult for some, if not all of them.

Jack nodded and pushed himself up straighter, grimacing at the movement. "They would be a welcome sight, Tim. This is like a jailhouse. Worse, because I can't get up and about. Or even eat a hearty meal."

"You sure took a pounding, Jack-O."

"I gave some back, though." He turned his fists over and glanced at the scabs on his knuckles. "That Brown will have some marks on him if they catch him."

"Don't hold your breath. Those boys have a head start and are likely far away by now. Sorry about your money, though. You'll win some more. Not from me, mind, but you will."

They both chuckled a bit, but Jack couldn't laugh much. For one thing, it still hurt. For another, he was still angry. Tim could see it disturbed Jack to be reminded of his lost winnings, so he changed the subject.

Lowering his voice, he looked toward the open door. "I hear that nurse is a darlin'. If I was you, I'd not be in such a hurry to vacate the premises."

"I'm sure I haven't noticed." Jack stifled a laugh.

"It's a good thing. And you all crippled up. No dancin' for you, not for a while yet." They were both giggling like schoolgirls by then. Suddenly, like a schoolmarm catching them misbehaving, Jillian walked in.

"What on earth are you two boys carrying on about? Mr. Fallon, you shouldn't be stressing your broken ribs."

She was carrying a pitcher of water, which she placed on the side table, retrieving the near-empty one. She turned to Jack and reiterated, "Having visitors is fine. They can help you forget your injuries. But don't get so rambunctious that you make them worse."

"Yes, ma'am," they said in unison, even though Tim's ribs were fine.

"This is Tim Kearney," said Jack. "He works with me at the mine."

"Yes, I remember. You were here with the sheriff that day."

"Yes, ma'am. Our Jack looked a sight then. Still does, though not so much."

Even Tim's head felt light just talking to her. He was immediately sorry inside for insinuating anything untoward with Jack. This was one kindhearted woman, but beautiful enough to take your breath away.

If I ever break a bone and end up in here, I'll surely be in trouble.

Jillian bid them goodnight and cautioned Jack to get some sleep.

They talked about everyday things from the mine for a while longer, but Jack started to lag in the conversation. Since the time he woke up in the hospital, he had had trouble staying awake for long periods. Tim replaced his chair and picked up his hat.

"You do whatever they tell you to get well, Jack. And you can tell us all about that nurse when you get back."

He laughed, and Jack just nodded, too resistant to such thoughts in his condition.

15

JACK WAS NEVER ONE TO TAKE A NEGATIVE VIEW OF life, but this was luck at its worst. He awoke this morning with the same thought he had each morning here: If he didn't get back to work soon, he doubted his chances of retaining any job with the company, no matter what this nurse told him Mr. Kelley had said.

On the other hand, this particular nurse was certainly worth staying in the hospital for. Jack had had a few female acquaintances, though none more serious than providing luck on his arm at card games here and there. Surely none that made him consider risking his job, not to mention life and limb.

The subject of his thoughts breezed in with yet another pitcher of water and a towel.

"You're awake. How do you feel, Mr. Fallon?" Jillian set the pitcher and towel on Jack's side table and leaned close to judge the progress of his facial wounds.

"Much better now. Thank you." Although his face was still somewhat swollen, at least he could speak more clearly than before. In truth, he still felt like he'd fallen down the shaft, but it's amazing what a tonic fresh beauty can be to a young man wanting to be up and about.

Much better now that you're here. When I get out of here, I'll find a way to get back here, and not as a patient.

She poured a glass of water. As she handed it to Jack, their fingers touched. He imagined a spark between them, but then he saw a modest gold wedding band. Jack was crestfallen.

"You… You're married?"

Jillian looked at him as if he had asked what color is the sky. "I am. Why?"

"I beg your pardon. I just didn't know. I mean, I just saw your hand and, well, I've not been myself lately. I hope I haven't said—"

"What *are* you prattling on about? Yes, I'm married. You are under my husband's care. Doctor Brandt is in charge of this hospital, and I am the nurse. Whatever you might have been thinking, Mr. Fallon, you probably shouldn't."

She wasn't angry, mostly surprised. But she thought it best to put some space between them for the afternoon and let the orderly on duty take care of anything he might need. Without another word, she finished fussing with his pillow and sheets, poured him some more water, and left him alone.

Jack was in shock. Married!

He tried to remember if he had indeed said anything inappropriate in his weakened mental state. She was a striking woman, and he was never a rowdy, flirtatious sort, but he had to admit he might have been tempted if he hadn't been so badly hurt. He was just beginning to feel well enough to see her as a woman, but unfortunately for him, he picked the wrong woman. Married to his doctor, no less. Why, he could find himself on the receiving end of a lethal dose of something nasty, and no one would be the wiser, since it would be the selfsame doctor who would have to determine the cause of death.

Watch yourself, Jack. And forget anything about this woman.

At about the time Jack reached the decision to mind his manners and his own business regarding Mrs. Brandt, he heard footsteps coming down the hall. During the day, his door was left wide open, Jillian said it was to keep the air healthy. She did not say that the doctor had ordered it so. And the doctor did not say to either of them that he ordered it so because he did not trust the young man to keep his hands and eyes to himself while Jillian administered to his wounds.

Jack listened as the footsteps drew closer, and he did not wonder why his heartbeat quickened in anticipation. At the same time, he tried to push such feelings down deep before they became troublesome. Despite his own reluctance, he still wished she weren't already married. He had been a loner until now, but he had a whole life ahead of him—why not share it with someone else?

The footsteps in the hallway paused as Han Liu peeked around the doorjamb. In one jumbled thought, Jack was glad it wasn't Jillian, but forced the disappointment from his mind.

He motioned Han into the room. Han hesitantly stepped into the doorway, and Jack waved him closer. "I hear you're the one to thank for getting me here. Thank you."

Han looked relieved and bowed slightly. "Welcome. Sorry, my English is not good."

"Don't you worry," said Jack, "I don't speak English, either. I'm Irish."

"Sorry?" said Han again, puzzlement returned to his face.

Jack waved him off, deciding he would find some time to try to help Han with his English, if he wanted it, though it sounded very good so far. Maybe they would become friends. He certainly owed him more than that, but he would find some way to repay the young man. Since coming to America, Jack couldn't find it in himself to treat the Chinese like some people did, as lower human forms and objects of scorn. To Jack, they were fellow immigrants in circumstances similar to his own. True, they were harder to understand, harder even than the Finns or Italians he had met in his travels, but to Jack, "different" didn't necessarily mean bad.

Jack pointed to himself. "I am Jack."

"Han." He smiled back.

Jack held out his hand to shake, and Han looked puzzled again and stayed by the doorway.

Most white men do not shake hands with Celestials, and this one doesn't know how to act. Well, I'm not going to be 'most white men' to this fellow who saved my life.

Jack waved Han closer to his bedside, reached for Han's right hand with both of his, and shook it slowly.

"Glad to know you, Han," he said.

Han shook Jack's hand back vigorously.

"Listen, Han, when I get out of here, we'll get together. I owe you my life, you know."

Han was unsure why or how they would ever "get together," given their drastically different backgrounds, but he could hear the sincerity in Jack's voice. He only nodded in feigned understanding.

"So, you're the laundry man around here?"

"Yes. Well, one," said Han. "Family has a laundry."

"I know. I mean, I know about the laundry. I've brought you my business now and then—I just don't remember you."

"Maybe Father or brothers. But thank you."

By then, Jack's eyelids felt heavy, and he yawned.

"Sorry, Han. I sleep a lot. My head, you know." He settled himself back into the pillow. Jack's eyes closed, and his breathing slowed. Han quietly left.

16

AS THE DAYS PASSED, JACK GREW IMPATIENT WITH lying in the hospital bed all day with nothing to keep his mind occupied. Instead of sleeping much of the day and night, he was restless. Jillian had left him a couple of books to read, but they were a little above him, so his attention wandered. His strength was returning, and his headaches were less severe, so he hoped he would be leaving soon to return to the mine. He wondered if he would have to start again at the bottom of the ladder, mucking underground.

The more Jack tried to convince himself not to think about Nurse Brandt, the less success he had. When a young man has little else to occupy him, and lying in a bed all day gives little distraction indeed, his mind is capable of all flights of imagination.

"Oh, but this is a losing game, Jack boy," he whispered to himself.

And as if his thoughts alone summoned her, Jillian appeared at his open door, knocking twice with a formality that was hardly needed after all this time. She walked in with a tray holding his lunch.

"Good afternoon, Mr. Fallon." She set the tray on his bedside table and began setting things for his meal.

"Good afternoon, Mrs. Brandt," said Jack, feeling silly with all the formal manners, and still believing she had seen him in a much less formal state.

Jillian had not yet admitted it was the orderly who had undressed him. It was her private joke to herself, and it helped to keep things professional, though less serious, between them.

"Soup again," he said. "It feels like I'm in jail. When can I get up and eat real food?"

"This is easier on your digestion when you're not leading an active lifestyle as you used to."

"And how'm I ever going to get back to that 'lifestyle' if I'm wastin' away to nothing?"

"Doctor Brandt says you'll be leaving us just as soon as you're able to manage walking without fainting. You had a serious concussion, and the head is slower to heal than the rest of your bones—hard as it is."

She smiled at that brief moment of chiding conversation. For a moment, Jack felt light-headed again, as if he had stood up too fast.

If her smile is making me swoon, I'd better get back amongst my fellows or I'll surely be done for.

"Now, finish your lunch, and I'll be back later," said Jillian.

"Yes, ma'am."

Then she was gone. Jack dove into his soup and bread roll and tried to concentrate on not spilling his food. An unsteady hand would be another sure sign of his slow healing. Soup stains on his bed sheets, a dead giveaway. He had one job now: to get well enough to put himself far away from this hospital and its distractions.

Rays of the afternoon sun inched across the floor and crept up the wall. Jack's eyes were closed when Jillian returned a few hours later to pick up his dishes. As quietly as she could, she set everything on his tray but reached across him to smooth a lock of his hair off his face.

She had a fleeting thought: if only she had met this man at a different time. Then, turning away, she picked up the tray, and the soup bowl rattled a bit.

Jack opened his eyes at the soft sound of her starched clothing and tinkling dishes. "Do you have to go right away?" he asked sleepily. "I'm tired of sleeping all the time."

Jillian beheld the innocent, just-awake look in his eyes and hesitated. The shape of his face had long since returned to normal, and its kindness was hard to resist.

"Well, I've no duties here with you just now. I really should—" She felt as though she were trying to hold a door shut against the wind.

"And none elsewhere either, so I've heard. There are no other patients in the house?"

"Well, no, not really. I—"

Jack looked down at his hands for a moment, as if trying to come to a decision. He smoothed his bedsheet while gathering his thoughts, and then admitted.

"I've a confession to make, and don't think it's some line I've said to anyone else. As I've been lying here all these days, I know I need to get well and get back to work, back to my life."

Before he could stop himself, the rest tumbled out.

"But don't take it to mean anything forward, because I do accept that you're the wife of my own doctor, but I must confess there's almost as much incentive to want to stay right here, what with you coming and going and asking after me day in and day out."

Jack felt his face flush, though he fought to keep from smiling at the weight being lifted from his mind.

"Oh, I'm rambling on, and please don't take it for anything. I'm better all the time, and I'll be gone as soon as I'm able. I just wanted to get that off my chest." He feigned a serious expression. "In my weakened state, you understand. Before I grew strong enough to resist."

They both giggled.

Jillian felt the color rise in her own cheeks. She pursed her lips and tried to put on a stern face. "I'll take your state of mind and body into consideration, Mr. Fallon."

"Jack."

"Yes. Jack it is."

She tightened her grip on the tray of dishes and headed for the door. It was becoming harder for her to trust herself to maintain her professionalism. The sooner he returned to work, the better.

"And I do have other duties somewhere, I'm sure."

She disappeared down the hall.

Jack let his head flop back on the pillow, and this time the swimming dizziness wasn't from his concussion.

Later that night, after his dinner, which had been brought by an orderly much to Jack's disappointment, and well after his lamp had been extinguished for the night, Jack listened to be sure there was no activity on his floor. Then he slowly sat up in bed. All felt perfectly normal, so he incrementally slipped his legs over the side of the bed, one at a time, and again took stock of his senses.

"In for a penny, boy-o," he whispered.

He very slowly rose to a standing position while holding onto the bed frame. He turned his head and glanced at his open door. *Well, that wasn't so ba—*

The blackness of the deepest mine ever burrowed suddenly fell over him, and he crashed to the floor.

Jack had no idea how long he lay there, but what little evening gloom he last saw out his window was long gone by the time he awoke. He felt for the bed and hauled himself back up into it after some stabbing pain from his half-healed ribs.

He tried to get comfortable again and cover himself. Nothing new hurt, and the old hurts were no worse than he would expect from lying around these many weeks. More importantly, his head no longer pounded and swam at the exertion of getting back into bed.

Well, that must be a good thing.

Doctor Brandt brusquely walked into Jack's room the next morning as the full day's sun filled the room, and without so much as a "Good morning," he examined Jack's eyes as they fluttered open from the most restful sleep he'd had in the hospital.

Jack startled at Brandt's face so close, looking at him as if Jack were a bug.

"What is it? Am I okay?"

"I would say you've recovered enough from your injuries, Mr. Fallon, to leave us soon. Maybe tomorrow," said Brandt. "How is your breathing?"

"My chest doesn't hurt as bad as it did." That was mostly true, but when he coughed, it still felt like being stabbed in his sides.

"Dizziness?"

"No," Jack lied. He didn't feel like recounting his midnight attempt at standing. The need to return to work wasn't the only reason he felt compelled to leave, and for his own good.

Brandt stepped back and looked at Jack with a half frown, like he was a rat caught in a trap. In Jack's imagination, somehow Brandt knew everything Jack had thought and said to his wife.

"Well, tomorrow then," Dr. Brandt said. "I'll look you over again and inform Mr. Kelley you're fit enough for light work. Nothing down in the pit, mind you. Not for a while, anyway. Keep your chest wrapped tightly as you can and change it every day. For at least a month."

He turned and left. The doctor's bedside manner was gruff and businesslike, and there was no kindness in his face. Jack didn't expect any and was ready to be done with the good doctor as soon as he could.

That night, as he had on a few other nights in the quiet, near-empty hospital, Jack heard arguing in the living quarters above. He couldn't make out actual words, but he knew a good fight when he heard one. He had to assume it was Jillian and the doctor. He knew there were no other patients and that the Brandts had an apartment upstairs. Also, that the orderlies all left for the day after sundown. It pained him to know theirs was not a happy marriage by any stretch.

17

THE TEMPORARY LOSS OF ONE LABORER HAD NO impact on the steady flow of silver ore down the mountainside, suspended in the company's cable trams. Ore from the tunnels left the mine on a gravity-driven tram that stretched almost two miles down the mountain to the mill down in Rumsey. Another cable serviced the mill in Philipsburg, bringing many tons of ore every hour to be crushed in stamp mills and processed into silver.

An army of laborers like Jack worked toward the final goal: producing heavy ingots of cast silver and delivering them to the railroad platform in Philipsburg to be shipped out. Silver flowed out while money flowed in. A share of the money, at least—the St. Louis investors saw most of it.

In the upstairs offices of the Miners' Union Hall, superintendent Thomas Weir leaned forward in his chair, facing a huge desk behind which sat the top three local union bosses. President Gilfillen was flanked by his vice-president, Anthony Towne, and Mickey Donovan, union treasurer. Towne was nearly as heavy as Gillfillen but younger and more solid. He was known as someone who would convince others of the wisdom of the president's wishes if need be. Donovan was tall and thin, bearded, and more bookish, befitting his position.

In Weir's hand was a telegram he'd received that morning from St. Louis. It was his job to maintain the mine's output at peak levels, and his whole life as a manager had been a successful one. But for the first time, he was in a quandary, and these men could make or break the future of everyone on the mountain.

"Gentlemen, I have here a telegram from St. Louis."

No further clarification was necessary. "St. Louis" referred to their financial backers, supporting the entire company. Edicts handed down from on high affected each of them and their union members.

"No doubt you are acquainted with current events surrounding the dangerous price of silver, and the unfortunate effect it has had on mines all over the nation." He took a deep breath, "Well, the investors have decided to discontinue operations for the time being—"

"For the time being?" interrupted Jimmy Gilfillen. "What does that mean, Thomas? The mine is shutting down?"

"Now don't get excited—"

"The boys aren't going to stand for losing their jobs, Mr. Weir," Anthony Towne said. "You can count on some trouble over this."

Weir had wrestled with this growing anxiety long enough and was no longer interested in easing into the dark news. The sooner they accept what's coming, the better they can help prepare for it.

"Listen, men, when the money stops, the hoist stops. I can tell you the government has scuttled the price of silver, and it's nobody's fault here on this mountain. But I promise you, I will keep as many men working as I can, as long as the accounts last. But know this: we're all about to be farmers."

Gilfillen recalled his last conversation with Weir and his promise to keep things under control. He looked at the other union men and sighed. "Strikes won't help us this time, boys. We all need to try and remain calm, and for God's sake, keep the fellows calm. Remember what the Butte men did recently? We don't want that here."

In Butte, there had been some union troubles unrelated to silver prices, and three troublemakers used some stolen dynamite from the company's own powder house to blow up an important piece of the workings. One man was accidentally killed, and work was halted for three days while the mine yard was cleared of debris. The company had refused to pay any of them during the halt.

"We can wind this down peaceably and help each other," Weir said, "and our members—your members—to pick up and live on. There'll be some dark times, but I believe this city has guts enough to stand up to it."

Weir stood up. "In the meantime, I'm telling Tom Kelley to cease operations on third shift. He'll move as many men as he can find work for to the first and second shift, or offer them to cash out plus a day's pay if they'll leave."

The union men grew angry and pounded their chair arms. They all grumbled at once.

Gilfillen rose. "That's a terrible thing to do! Some of these are family men! They can't just pick up on a half-week's pay and go God knows where. The other companies down the mountain are nowhere near able to absorb so many men. The other silver mines will be closing, too."

"Jimmy, I'm trying to do the best I can for the most men. I'm sorry. We'll keep going as long as we can, but start working on your membership to think in terms of moving on."

He turned to leave amid grousing and hissing among the union bosses. He knew as well as they that he was only the bringer of bad news.

As he left the union hall, he thought of all the improvements he had made to their working conditions, but all that, he felt, was about to be wiped away as word spread that the mine was closing.

They won't remember all the good—only the bad news, and the messenger who brought it.

18

NURSING WAS A NOBLE CALLING. JILLIAN BELIEVED that relieving the suffering of others was one of the greatest gifts one could give. Her abilities at the Granite hospital had luckily never been overwhelmed, as patients came infrequently, and few required longer-term care than a day or two. New mothers sometimes needed time to heal before starting their own full-time job of mothering. Injured miners were patched up and sent back to work as soon as possible. Common diseases took a toll, of course, and death was a frequent visitor.

But at any given time, she had many hours of the day with little to do but study to improve her skills, and to reflect on the purpose of her life in this place and time.

To be married at nineteen, a woman has no opportunity to learn the possibilities the world holds. She was happy with her life in her first few years as the wife of the town doctor. If he had a temper, well, who could blame him?

Life was hard in the mines, and Jillian imagined it was harder still for a doctor in a town far removed from modern advances in medicine available in big cities. Operating rooms, with all the latest appliances and professional nursing staff, meant the odds of surviving accidents or disease were much greater.

Robert did the best he could under the circumstances, Jillian rationalized, and if he got angry when people died whom he could otherwise have saved, then she would just have to help him through the pain of what he perceived as his own failure.

However, these last few years, he had become increasingly short-tempered. With no frame of reference but her own life, she believed it was just part of married life. But she wondered, *Is this what I have to look forward to?*

Life has its ups and downs. Now, though she refused to consider that it had anything to do with the young man in her care, Jillian was having other thoughts. Questioning whether her life was truly a prison sentence, or if she was eligible for parole.

She had many conversations with herself, arguing whether she should just accept her fate or if she could find a better life off the mountain. Somewhere brighter, where her life didn't depend on the suffering or sweat and toil of others.

She was in that frame of mind one day as Robert happened to launch into one of his dark moods. She was arranging some of the medical implements in the intake and examination room when he stormed in.

"This is work for an orderly. Can't you find some work suited to your abilities?"

"Robert, there is nothing else to do at the moment. Joseph is filling the woodshed. Or would you rather I did that?"

Brandt grabbed her forearm and spun her around to face him, so violently that she felt her shoulder strain. She cried out.

After a stern look into her face, Robert let go. "Don't be flippant! It's not my fault that there are no patients lately." His eyes narrowed. "Except for your Fallon boy."

"Don't be absurd. I give him no more attention than any other patient. You've no reason to think—"

He grabbed her by both shoulders and squeezed her arms so tightly that she winced again in pain.

"Don't tell me what to think," he whispered. "I know what I know. If for one moment I thought you were unfaithful…"

Without another word, he left the room.

Jillian held herself tightly to keep from bursting into tears, but the room swam as her eyes threatened to over-flow. Her throat grew tight, and she fought to remain silent, clenching her mouth. Her breath hitched, and she felt herself falling again into a dark self-pity that knew no relief.

She realized that her marriage was not the fairy tale life she had imagined as a little girl. Her mother had told her to marry a rich man, a doctor perhaps. Well, she had, and now she regretted it. As many times as she had tried to make excuses, hoping things would improve, they instead grew worse.

That simple word, "regret," flitted through her mind more and more lately.

Divorce was almost unheard of. *I don't even know anyone who got divorced.* The reasons for divorcing someone were usually settled very privately. Or violently. The stigma generally forced one or both parties to relocate to another town and start fresh without any friends or family for support.

The loneliness of starting over kept many sad wives in miserable circumstances.

The thought of lashing out never occurred to her. The best possibility, though the notion would never occur to her, would have been a tragic accident or illness that might take Robert out of her life.

Until then, she had to simply live as best she could: concentrate on work and not let Robert's temper drag her down. And above all, keep her fantasies to herself.

19

AFTER HIS FIRST NIGHT IN HIS OWN BED BACK AT the Headley boarding house, Jack woke with a start. It was so quiet outside that he almost thought he was still asleep. When one gets accustomed to the noises of the normal hustle and bustle of a city, its absence can be deafening.

The company had reduced shifts even further, to one a day instead of round the clock. The familiar saying "Nothing ever stops in Granite" was no longer accurate. The machinery up at the mine and the mills below had been reduced to bankers' hours, with only the day shift bringing enough ore to the surface to operate half the stamp mills.

With fewer shifts, Jack had more free time than he was used to, especially since he was still on light work per the doctor's orders. Each morning, he was only required to check in at the company office to see if there was anything he could do. Kelley never told him what Superintendent Weir had said about Jack's job being secure, so usually, the answer was no.

With so many men being let go, Jack found it mysterious that he was not among them. He found the nerve to ask

Mr. Kelley about it and learned that Mr. Weir himself had made "allowances" due to Jack's injuries. He was grateful, though he suspected that day was coming for all of them.

On his return to work, rumors spread like wildfire that the mine might close altogether. The cutback in shifts was accompanied by news that silver was no longer a stable investment. Everyone was on edge, wondering if this was a temporary storm or a permanent change. Ever since he had begun planning a serious future in the saloon business, Jack had been thinking of how to accumulate the money he would need. The Granite mine paid well, but now that was in jeopardy. Some of the men had already left for greener pastures, and Jack was balancing the need for reliable income against an unacknowledged alternative: Jillian Brandt. The more he resisted thinking about her at all, the less he could concentrate on anything else.

He used his free time to wander about the town, hoping he might, with any luck, innocently cross paths with his nurse. His usual route took him from his room to the Miner's Union Hall, where most of his friends spent their off time, and down Main Street, still a busy place even as commerce lagged behind the dwindling number of people spending money.

On this day, luckier than any card game, he spied Jillian coming toward him on the opposite side of the street, carrying a basket of groceries.

He took a chance and angled across to meet her.

She paused and shifted her basket to her other arm. "Good morning, Mr. Fallon."

"Good morning to you, and I thought we had got past that."

He reached out and lifted the heavy basket from her arms. She didn't protest, a fact he also noted with satisfaction.

"Manners are a bad habit, I suppose."

She smiled a bit, then glanced up and down the street. He thought she was looking for anyone watching them.

"Don't worry. I doubt anyone notices two people having a conversation."

"Oh, it's not that," she said. Another fact he noted: she immediately knew he meant the two of them speaking together, and she felt self-conscious about it. "The town just seems different. Like we're in a copy that's only pretending to be itself, but not very convincingly."

"The town is dying, Jillian. Can't you feel it? The mine is shut at night, and the mills. And everything goes quiet. People are moving away. It's emptying out like a leaky bucket. There's already two saloons boarded up, and the barbershop too."

"We have plenty of saloons."

"True enough. But it won't be long now."

They walked back toward the hospital. Jack set the pace, as slow as he could, so he could spend some time with her. Just a few minutes here and there. He refused to think any farther ahead than that.

"So, tell me about Ireland, Jack."

"Ah," he thought for a moment. "Green."

"Pardon?"

"Green as far as you can see. Not like the green here with these pine trees—dark green. I mean, grass green. Ireland is rolling hills and open country."

She could see by his face that he was remembering the open spaces of his homeland.

"And old. The houses and shops, and farms are older than anywhere. Hundreds of years. Here in America, everything is new and modern. Why, look at the shops here. I'll bet none of this was here fifty years ago. Twenty years ago."

Jillian laughed. "Less than that, Jack."

"Ay. Newly cut and milled. You can smell it. There's hardly a tree left on this mountain to get under in the rain. They've all been cut down for lumber and firewood, and shoring for the mines. Don't misunderstand, I'm all for using what's needed, but this place has a hurry-up-and-get-rich taste to it."

"You should be glad. It's why you have a job."

"True again. It brought me here." *Take the plunge, Jack.* "It brought me to you, too."

The reactions passed over her face all at once: eyes widening, then a bit of reluctance, lips pressed together in the start of refusal—but just beyond it, the faintest hint of the "maybe" he was hoping to see.

"Jack, you shouldn't think… Just because I did my job and nursed you back to health… Well, you need to understand, patients often form attachments."

He could tell she didn't really believe her own words. He knew he shouldn't meddle in a person's personal affairs, especially a marriage. But it pained him to see it. He really did believe she deserved more.

"I can't help what I think, Jillian. I'm trying, believe me, I am. I know what's what in this world. And I'll be back at the mine for as long as I'm able. Then I'll go, like everyone else. I surely don't mean to come between you and what you deserve. And you deserve to be happy. And I don't mean with me. Not at all."

He thought twice at that.

"Well, not necessarily with me."

He looked into her eyes and held her gaze. "You are a fine, kind, honest person. Full of life and a welcoming spirit to the world. I hope you find contentment."

She had no answer to that. What could she say? Her own conflict was buried deep within, and despite the growing closeness with this man, she couldn't entertain any alternative.

They stopped at the crossroads in front of the church. The hospital was a little further down the road toward Philipsburg.

"I should probably disappear," said Jack.

She only reached to take back her basket of food.

"Thank you. For carrying my things, I mean. And for the company, Jack."

She left so much unsaid. They both knew it. He only tipped his cap and gave her one last serious look before he turned back up Main Street.

Deep in thought, he meandered back to Broadway toward his room, but changed his mind and decided to visit Han Liu at the laundry. Han had visited Jack several times in the hospital, just stopping by to say hello, and Jack was touched by his genuine concern. But it was time he did something for the fellow who saved his life.

As he stepped up on the plank front porch of the laundry, Han came around the corner of the building. "Mr. Jack!"

"Hello, Han," Jack said. "You don't need to call me mister."

"Ah, but it is respect for elders. My parents are very strict."

Jack laughed. "Elders? I'm not that much 'elder' than you."

They both entered the front of the shop, and Han looked closely at Jack's face.

"You look much better now. That day, oh boy, you scared us sure."

"Yes, I'm a little sore yet, but on the mend." Han seemed to be between chores, so Jack got to the point. "Han, I still want to repay you somehow for helping me. I've just never…"

"Jack. If you see me lying on the road, what do you do?"

"Well, of course, I'd—"

Han interrupted, "Yes. Samey-same, Jack. The right thing is the right thing, no matter who."

"Alright, but my conscience won't let it be. What about your English? Or reading and writing? You sure speak it well enough."

"Thank you. The school here is very good. My brothers are still learning, but they are young. My parents, not much English at all. I help with papers and things. We have relatives down in the other town, I help them, too."

Jack saw an opening. He had only seen Han's pushcart.

"That's a long walk. You have no wagon?"

"It is good to be healthy," Han said.

"That's it then. Han, how about this? Sometimes in my job—they won't let me work down the mine yet—I have to go down to town for this and that. I'm mostly a fetching boy now."

"Fetching?"

"'Jack, go get me this. Go get that.' Fetching things for the boss." Han nodded. "So, they have a wagon. Next time I'll stop by here and see if you need to go to town, and you can ride with me. How would that be?"

Han's eyes showed surprise and understanding all at once. He was humbled that Jack would make the offer and, at the same time, glad that they had become acquainted. Four miles was indeed a long walk, eight miles both ways, and his family usually had to wait until the hike was worth the effort as well as the time lost from work, no matter the purpose of the trip.

"Jack, that is most kind. I would be happy to ride and not walk. But I would not want you to be in trouble."

"Fear not, lad," Jack said imperiously. "When I'm captain o'the wagon, I say who rides in it."

They both laughed, and the deal was sealed.

Outside in the working side of the house, voices were raised in commotion, but all in Chinese.

Han said, "Back to work, Jack. And thank you."

"You betcha, Han. Be seeing you."

Jack returned to the mine office to see if any "fetching" needed to be done. As busy as he kept himself, the light, menial labor left his mind to wander back to Jillian and her predicament. He was sure she did not view it as a "predicament," just an unhappy situation she was resigned to. But with no one else to help her out of it, what kind of life was that?

A totally illogical fantasy began to take root in which the two of them, with nothing here to hold them—he, soon to be without a job, and she, with no viable future in a marriage to an abusive husband—escaped together. He wasn't entirely sure if she had those kinds of feelings, about escaping or about him, but he knew for certain that he was far past beginning to have them for her.

A daily train on the spur line out of Philipsburg ran up to the Union Pacific line in Drummond, about twenty-five miles to the north. It brought freight, food, down, and freshly smelted ingots of silver back up, on their way east to St. Louis.

Jack believed that if he and Jillian rode that train, they could go anywhere in the world.

Some large city far away where no one would know them, Seattle, maybe. There would be plenty of work there for a willing young man, though probably not mining work, which would be fine with Jack. With Jillian in his life, mining would no longer be the sunrise and sunset of his existence.

Then the little bird named The Green Isle Saloon alighted on Jack's shoulder and whispered, "What about me?"

The choice seemed impossible: Jillian or his gambling emporium. The two notions rolled round and round, until he considered, *why decide between them?* His saloon was in the future. Jillian was here and now. It was a fact that he would continue working, no matter where, and eventually he would get back to his card-playing for some real money. All his extra savings could still build his casino someday. In the meantime, his life would be more fulfilling with Jillian by his side. If she would have him.

None of his musings were worth the time if she wasn't willing to make her escape with him. Even if she wanted nothing more than his help getting out of her dead-end life. If that was the case, he would give all the help she asked, then say his goodbyes. But he hoped she would eventually feel more for him. She was too close to see it for herself, but that doctor was no kind benefactor.

20

EARLY THE NEXT DAY, MINE MANAGER KELLEY CAME downstairs from the union offices to find Jack and Tim Kearney in the Union Hall bar. At that time of day, a man could grab a quick, simple breakfast at the Hall, and both men were eating egg sandwiches between turns at the billiard table. Jack was trying, without success, to learn billiards despite Kearney's expert demonstration. Truth be told, Kearney was hoping to teach Jack just to be good enough to play, but bad enough so that Kearney might win some of that eighty-seven dollars he knew Jack had hidden away to gamble with.

The investors had sent Thomas Weir a strongly worded letter instructing him to provide a timetable for when the mine would close altogether, as well as a date when no further funds would be needed for supplies and wages. Weir and Kelley resigned themselves to the mine's inevitable closure and had worked out a schedule with the union bosses, leading to the last payment of all bills and wages by the end of the week. Kelley stuffed their handwritten reply into a Western Union envelope.

"Kearney!" he yelled, "Take this telegram down to town at once. Don't stop for any—"

"My shift starts in an hour, boss. Should I tell the foreman?"

"No. Um…" Kelley turned to Jack. "Fallon?"

"Jack Fallon, yes, sir."

"Fallon, take this—Uh, when does your shift start?"

"I'm still on light duty, sir. No worries."

"Right. Take this envelope to the train station down in town. Have them wire it immediately on the company account. And don't stop for anyone or anything, understand?"

"Yes, sir."

Kelley rushed back upstairs, still mumbling to himself. If the union bosses could keep their heads just a little longer, the company might avoid trouble. There was a considerable amount of valuable machinery and tools left to bring out of the mine and prepare for shipment to other company-owned properties, and they needed to keep men on the payroll long enough to do it. Some had left already because of shutdown rumors.

"What do you suppose has him in such a twist?" Jack asked Kearney.

"I dunno, Jack boy, but if I was you, I'd get down to town."

Jack picked up his hat from the bar and started toward the door. He stuffed the envelope in his jacket and stuffed the remains of his egg sandwich into his mouth.

Kearney growled out behind him, in a pretty good Kelley imitation, "And don't you be stoppin' for nobody, Fallon."

They both laughed as the door slammed.

Jack went immediately to the company office to borrow the wagon for his mission to town, but McFeeney told him it was already down in Philipsburg on another errand. So Jack set off downhill on foot.

The road from Granite down to Philipsburg was usually a bustling byway of wagons and people walking the four miles up and down between the two towns. Jack made the trip to town on foot many times in his months at Granite, and was always at his most careful at the curves. Some were dangerous to take on foot, as draymen had enough trouble wrestling their teams on the hill without having to watch for pedestrians. A person could generally hear the crunch of metal-shod wagon wheels on the hard dirt road soon enough to get to the side and avoid being crushed. On occasion, he could hitch a ride up or down if the drover was in the mood or if he was an acquaintance from the company.

More adventurous hitchhikers would jump onto a passing tram bucket near one of the tramway towers and ride most of the way in style, suspended over the hillside like a king and enjoying the view. But it was against company rules as a safety violation, and getting caught meant you drew your last wages.

On this day, traffic was light and only a few carts passed in either direction. The fading town had little need for the supplies and freight it once did.

The sun was climbing higher in the morning sky, and the fragrant mountain air filled his lungs. Jack let his thoughts drift, as they had more frequently of late, to Jillian and her sad life at the hospital. Marriages were most often a permanent state of being, and anything that interrupted them other than death was cause for scandal among neighbors and strangers alike. Jack did not picture himself as a home-wrecker, nor would he even think to bring such ill repute to a woman as fine and upstanding as Jillian.

He could not, however, understand why a woman as smart and talented as she would suffer herself to remain in the company of a man as abusive as the doctor. *A doctor yet.* A man who commits his life to helping people, to healing people, and relieving pain. Yet he inflicts the greatest pain and anguish on a woman he is supposedly in love with, so much so that he would spend the rest of his life in her company. And she, so obedient that she couldn't imagine any alternative.

It just didn't make sense to Jack that she should stay with such a lout.

As if the angels had been reading his thoughts, around the bend behind him came a buckboard wagon driven by none other than Jillian herself. Jack stepped back against the uphill side of the road with his back to the rocks and whipped off his cap just as she noticed who it was.

She reined her horse to a stop. "Good morning," she said.

Jack smiled so broadly he could almost taste his ears. "And good morning to you, too."

Her smile was as bright as the morning and a bit past cordial, or so he imagined. He hoped. If anyone had been watching, the look on their faces was as if they had been searching and just found each other in a crowd.

"You're headed down to town?" she asked.

"Yes, ma'am. To the telegraph office at the train station."

"If I don't make you sit in the back, would you like a ride? I'm going the opposite way down on Broadway, but I can drop you at the station."

Jack was halfway up to the seat before she finished speaking. "Thank you, kindly. It sure will save time. And it looks to be a hot climb back up…" Hinting that he hoped for a return trip.

Jillian click-clicked the horse back into motion, and Jack settled himself beside her at a respectable distance.

She nodded at the Western Union envelope sticking out from Jack's breast pocket. "Wiring your riches to the Bank of England?"

"Ha! I'd sooner slit my own throat as wire anything to the Bank of England. Besides, my 'riches' would hardly pay for the wire itself." He drew the envelope from his pocket and held it up to the light. "No. This is from the mine manager, Kelley, to the company back east, I think. See? It says 'Granite Mountain Mining Company, St. Louis.'"

"They're probably begging the company to keep the mine open a little longer. It's so sad. So many men have lost their jobs," she said.

"Sad indeed. Some of the other mines down the valley are shutting down, too. We're lucky to be open this long. Many of the men have already gone. Families, too. They have to go where the work is. I suppose I'll be leaving soon, too."

He looked straight ahead but strained to feel how she reacted to his leaving. He looked sideways to try and see her face, but there was little reaction to see.

This is silly. She has her life, such as it is, and I've got no cause to think she should feel one way or the other about whether I stay or go or jump in a lake.

Jillian had almost the identical thoughts, though she could hardly admit them to herself, let alone to the man riding with her in the wagon. But any woman can hold onto a dream down deep.

Jack mustered his courage and decided to go for broke. The opportunity was evaporating the closer they came to the end of the ride, and with only days until he would really have to leave, Jack knew the time for serious talk was now.

"Do you recall the confession I made to you before?" he asked. "When I was still in the hospital?"

Jillian had replayed that conversation so many times, she knew it by heart. Of course, she remembered. It had lifted her up each time, and then she always came crashing back to her real life.

How can something make you feel so good and leave you so sad at the same time?

She didn't trust herself to speak, as her throat was tight, so she only nodded.

"Well, I know what's 'proper,' and how gentle folks should act and all. Folks like you. And the doctor, I guess. I'm not what you'd call a 'gentleman,' but I'm a workin' man, and I see things. I also know what's right and what's wrong. Jillian, I've heard you and the doctor a few times in the apartment upstairs. Not the words, mind you. I'd cut off my ears rather than eavesdrop on anyone. But I heard the tone, and I have to say it's plain to see yours is not a model marriage."

"Jack—"

He held up his hand. "I apologize, because I know it's not my place, but I can't leave here thinking of you living out your life like this. There must be someone, some family of yours, some place you could be happier. Can't you just go and start up fresh somewhere else?"

Whether I'm in the picture or not, she deserves better.

"Jack…" She took a deep breath. "To answer your question, no, I've no family. My parents are both passed, buried down in Philipsburg. But I appreciate your concern. I'll be alright." Inside, she screamed at herself for the lies she was telling. "The work presses on him sometimes, of course. But if the mine closes…"

"*When* the mine closes," he said.

"Yes. When the mine closes, Robert won't have to work so hard, and we'll be fine."

Jack rested his hand on her forearm.

"Jillian, when the mine closes, the work you're speaking of will disappear altogether. This town will go bust, and everyone in it will be gone. He'll gave no patients."

"Then we'll have no choice but to move on ourselves and survive."

"And how much stress will that put on him? And on your marriage? I hate to think of the rough road you'll have ahead."

They might not have another opportunity to talk alone before the mine, the town, and their lives spun apart forever. His desperation suddenly welled up inside him. He was finished being the helpful advice-giver. If he didn't jump in now, he might never have another chance.

He turned in his seat to face her fully.

"Like I said, I'm a workin' man. I've never wanted for a job, nor had trouble fending for myself. But, Jillian, I can fend for two as well as one. You're used to a better class of people, I know, but if you want to go, I can be the one to go with you. Even if you only want company and some protection until you reach another town, I'd make sure you got there safe. And if that's all, I'll say goodbye then. That day I woke up in the hospital, I thought you were an angel come to guide me home to heaven. I've never stopped feeling that way, and God strike me dead, I never will. I'm sorry if I've said too much, but I'd burst if I didn't. And with only days until we might never see each other again, my manners will just have to wait."

These same thoughts had grown deep inside her lately, at night and alone. As much as she tried to distract herself with her work, she kept coming back to the fact that she did deserve better. What's more, she believed Jack when he poured out his heart. The offer of only being a temporary protector solidified his honest intentions. She could feel her own heart stir at the thought of being together, only to part again forever, and the pain it would bring.

Her growing discontent at home was unconnected to the attentions of this handsome, though rough around the edges, Irishman. The flame in her marriage had flickered and gone out long before he arrived. But the realization was slowly dawning that, yes, she could indeed see a future with Jack.

She only nodded. It was unfitting to air her personal troubles. And she had few, if any, friends or acquaintances in whom she could confide during the dark times in her life. She was embarrassed enough that he, a perfect stranger, had noticed the situation between her and Robert, and she wondered if others had seen it, too, but were unwilling to speak to her about it. Until this moment, she believed she had successfully concealed her own despair from the world.

Jack's abruptness had certainly caught her attention. Opening that door only added to her uncertainty about what to do. She surely had some decisions to make, and soon.

They rode on in silence until the road leveled out close to town, where the trees closed in on both sides of the road as if trying to block their escape. At the lower altitude, the air warmed a bit. But the rocking of the wagon and the soft breeze of their forward motion reminded them that the uncertainty of Granite was far behind them.

As she steered through Philipsburg and maneuvered down the once-busy main street, they felt as though the wind was failing the ship. Even down here, some of the smaller shops and businesses had closed, with a board or two nailed across the front doors. Several smaller mines in the hills above Philipsburg were feeling the crunch of dwindling funds as well.

More than one heavy wagon was parked at the various shops and supply stores on Broadway, and the owners were piling their belongings on top.

Jillian stopped at one she knew, the Moffet's. Their little eight-year-old blonde-haired boy waited on the seat beside his mother, munching on an apple, as his father wrestled a barrel off the boardwalk and into the back of the wagon with the rest of their worldly possessions.

"Mrs. Moffet, you're leaving, too?" Jillian asked. "Where are you headed?"

"James wants to try Anaconda or maybe Butte. I hope they have jobs. Otherwise, I don't know…" She looked off into the distance.

"Well, good luck to all of you. We'll all be on the move soon, I suppose." She drove the wagon further down the street and shook her head.

"Everyone I know and care about is leaving, Jack. I've never felt so… I don't know… on the verge. It's like there's a cliff right in front of me, and if I take a step, I'll be lost."

Jack nodded. What more could he add? She now knew his position. He'd planted the seeds, and no matter which direction she chose, he hoped she would be better off.

21

THEY REACHED THE RAILROAD STATION AT THE lower end of Broadway. The tracks crossed the dusty, hard-packed street, and the long, narrow station sat end-on to the roadway and parallel to the tracks. There were piles of freight and luggage on the covered entrance platform, and several people, some with the sad, stoic faces of refugees, were milling about waiting for the next train. Jillian pulled up along the raised platform in front. Jack climbed down and held the horse's bridle. He looked up at Jillian. They both had furrowed brows.

"Think about what I said. You should be happy, Jillian. Happier, at least."

"I'm fine," she said.

Neither of them believed it.

Jack went into the station, and Jillian turned the wagon to head up to the Hope Mill at the other end of Broadway.

She saw no one else she knew, the mood in town mirroring her own. Her mind dwelt on the conversation with Jack. She began to actually believe she ought to have the life he described. Like the lives of happy people she saw around her, or used to see before this mine trouble started. People living contented lives, though she hadn't felt like them for some time. Certainly, it's not a sin to want that.

Meanwhile, Jack made his way around the suitcases and steamer trunks and into the station. There was a large waiting area with four long wooden benches, two on each side of an aisle that led to the ticket counter. High on the wall over the front door was an ornate clock, visible to the entire room. A wood-framed chalkboard was mounted on the wall showing arrival and departure times. He passed a family arguing about their baggage. The wife was near tears at having to leave so many of their possessions up on the mountain. As they passed out of Jack's hearing, the husband was telling her they couldn't afford to bring everything. Jack, as well as those nearby, tried not to overhear, but it was clear that many of them were in a similar circumstance.

He approached the counter and saw that tickets were sold at one end, and Western Union telegraph business was conducted at the other. Behind the counter, the station manager, Elliston Booker, sat on a high stool and was ticking off lines on a waybill. Jack saw he was concentrating on his paperwork, so he remained silent. Booker was an older man with a short dark beard just turning gray. His midnight–blue flat-topped cap bore the insignia of the Union Pacific Railroad. He nodded once at Jack and held up one finger for a moment, not wanting to lose count. Presently, he put down his pencil and came to Jack at the telegraph counter.

Jack slid the envelope across the counter. He had no idea what it contained.

His conversation with Jillian occupied his attention so completely that he hadn't even considered peeking at what it said. To Jack, it was simply another menial job that he took in stride until he could get back to real work and his friends.

"Mr. Kelley asks that this be sent as soon as possible on the Granite company account, please."

"Certainly. Let's see what we have in words."

The station manager, who also served as the telegrapher, which was common in small town rail stops, drew a sheet of paper from Jack's envelope, placed it beside a blank telegraph form, and counted the words to be sent.

"Well, this is somewhat lengthy, but Granite can afford it." He chuckled. "And it's not from Kelley, mister, it's from Thomas Weir himself. But I suppose you not knowing that means you've not read it. Good man."

His pencil bounced over the page as he whispered the number of words.

"And it's to St. Louis, so there's a distance charge, but that's fine. Next train's not due for a while, so I'll send it right now." He lowered his voice conspiratorially. "That's another charge for 'Urgent.'" He chuckled again. "I'll put it on Granite's account, no worries, mister."

"Thank you."

"I'm not one to gossip, but seeing as you haven't read this…"

"No, I didn't think it was polite," said Jack.

"Well, you strike me as a miner, and I'd think a miner would want to know if he's out of work."

That got Jack's attention.

"It says here you boys are done and closed as of this Friday."

Jack swallowed hard, but refused to show his shock. It was finally here. The mine was done.

"Yes, we know," he lied. "We all know. Thank you, though."

As he left the train station, the heavy wooden door swung closed behind him with a bang. He didn't notice. Walking down the platform to the street, Jack felt strange inside, like a decision he had been wrestling with had been made for him. The conversation he had just had with Jillian now took on a new sense of urgency.

He had known the mine was on the verge of closing. All the fellows were talking about it—down the pit, in the bars, at the Union Hall. He noticed the reduction in shifts, the removal of unused machinery—it was no secret. The only secret was when. The company had stayed relatively quiet about what was coming, obviously trying to avert a panic of men quitting all at once.

No matter. He was young, talented, and healthy. The world had a way of providing for such survivors. He was looking for a job when he found this one. When the time came, he would go back to looking again.

The time had come, but with it had come Jillian. Jack had fought to avoid dreaming about some way to stay with her, or to convince her to stay with him, but now the dreams came full steam ahead.

After Friday, he would be unemployed. He could leave when he wished. Whether he would leave alone or not, that was yet to be determined.

He started walking back up Broadway, deep in thought. It occurred to him that maybe he could intercept Jillian on her way back, and he began walking faster.

His thoughts were a jumble. Oh, the cards they were a'shufflin'.

22

THE HOPE MINE AND MILL BEGAN OPERATION soon after the Civil War, and the town that grew around it would eventually be called Philipsburg. Several mines in the foothills above the town sent ore to be processed at the Hope Mill, and the ready supply of labor kept the mines and the mill running. The mill sat at the end of Broadway, farthest from the train station, before the road narrowed and climbed into the hills. The main office was firmly built of stone with wooden gables and a roof with many angles and peaks. Other buildings were added as the mill grew. The ten stamps it contained drummed away at the ore, and Jill could hear their pounding as she got close.

One of the young laborers, Jacob Francisco, had lost an argument with a drive belt on one of the ore crushers six weeks ago. Men either learned how not to get hurt, or they learned how not to see the next sunrise, and Jacob was still on that learning curve. Dr. Brandt had set and wrapped his broken arm in a plaster cast during one of his regular trips to town, visiting patients, and today was Jacob's "coming out" party.

Jillian was here to cut off the cast with a pair of heavy cast-cutting scissors. Whatever the future of the mine held for everyone, there were still everyday needs to be met, patients to tend to. She forced herself to put her thoughts of Jack on a shelf and get on with her duties. She tied off her horse's reins at the hitching rail in front of the Hope Mill office, gathered up her doctor's bag, and walked into the mill office.

Once inside, it was easy to see why there were many additions to the structure. The office was crammed with a multitude of cabinets and desks overflowing with papers and production records. There were workbenches with tools, and a long coat rack where the workers on shift hung their street clothes. As Jillian closed the door behind her, a gray cat jumped down from a cabinet beside her to a bench and skittered away into the jumbled interior. She heard and felt the rumbling of the stamp mill back in the depths of the building.

Old sweat and stale smoke from a cold wood stove assaulted her nose as Edoardo Manelli, the mill supervisor, stood up behind his desk and came around to greet Jillian.

"Why, Mrs. Brandt. Good morning to you. I suppose you're here to see young Jacob?"

"You are correct, Mr. Manelli," she smiled, holding up her bag. "I've got a pair of shears he'll be happy to see."

"That's fine. I'll run in and bring him out to you. It's all dust and dirt back in the mill. I'll be right back with our boy."

Jillian watched the comings and goings on Broadway through the front window. She had lived here all her life and was used to the typical street traffic, but lately it seemed to be of one purpose. When the town was growing, people came and went all the time. Nowadays, people seemed to only leave.

Jack's words kept repeating in her thoughts. Was it possible the hospital itself would close? The town of Granite was wholly dependent on the mine. If the men left, the shops and businesses would have no reason to remain open. The bottling plant would close. The saloons would close. The newspaper would close, with no news to report. So many places would be closed, people would have no choice but to move away.

Why would there even need to be a hospital? Or a doctor?

Robert will have to find work somewhere else, or worse, take other work until he finds a position. But that would crush him even more.

The back door squeaked open with a cloud of dust and noise, and Jacob emerged from the mill interior. He held up his left arm, encased in a plaster cast that was nearly disintegrating after six weeks of banging around the mill. "Mrs. Brandt! Am I ever glad to see you?"

Jacob was only nineteen, but his tall body had grown thick from toiling at hard jobs. His wide grin stretched the freckles in his young face, and even though it was early in the day, his black curly hair was layered with rock dust.

"Jacob," she said, "It looks like you've been using your cast as a tool. You're lucky you didn't break your arm again."

"Yes, ma'am, that's true enough. It does get in the way."

He sat on a chair in front of Manelli's desk while Jillian withdrew her shears. After some cutting and twisting, she had the cast off in several pieces and tossed them in a trash bin nearby. She examined his pale arm and was satisfied with its healing.

"I'm glad to be rid of that thing, ma'am. Now I can get my work—"

"Jacob, you still need to be gentle with that arm for a few weeks. It's not used to hard work. Or maybe it is, but don't go overdoing it or you'll be back in another cast."

"Yes, ma'am. I'll be careful."

"Alright, Jacob, enough loafing about the office," said Manelli. "The rocks are a'waitin'."

"Yes, sir." He tipped his hat to Jillian and was gone.

She put her shears away, said goodbye to Edoardo, and climbed back up in her wagon.

Starting back down Broadway, it occurred to her for the first time that she had acquired some valuable skills in her nursing duties—skills that might allow her to find work of her own, should she require living wages. The possibility of fending for herself was both frightful and exciting. Finding a new life, with or without Jack, might really be possible. Of course, the two of them together would make for combined resources, but she was still reluctant to take that plunge.

As she reached Sansone Street, the turn to head back up to Granite, Jack came running up the street from the train station, wearing a wide grin. Without even asking this time, Jack climbed up into the front seat of the wagon.

Jillian started to feign a protest, but Jack's expression stopped her.

"Do you know what that telegram was?" he asked, keeping his voice low.

"How would I know what it said, Jack?" she said suspiciously. She slapped the reins, and the horse moved back toward Granite.

"The telegraph man told me. He had to read it, of course, so he told me." Jack paused so he would have her full attention. "The mine superintendent told St. Louis they've arranged the shutdown 'as instructed.' The mine will close. This Friday. My friends and I will be out of work. I bet this whole town will fold if there's no work."

His words did not match his demeanor. Jack seemed giddy, like it was Christmas morning and he had gotten what he asked for.

"I'm so sorry, Jack. But why are you so happy about such a thing?"

"Look, Jillian, in cards, sometimes you have to take a chance. Take a card, and you don't know what it will be. It could drain your pockets, or it could change your life. Have you thought about what I said before?"

She nodded. "A little. Okay, a lot, Jack."

She started to feel a little giddy herself. She stood at the edge of a precipice. The world she knew was behind her, safe as ever, or at least comfortable. Another world she had no idea about lay one step into the abyss.

He took a deep breath and touched her hand. "This is a chance, THE chance, Jillian. I've got no job now, or I won't, come Friday. But I've never had trouble finding work, that's not a worry. Next week I'll be moving on." He paused until she glanced at him. "I want you to come with me."

Jillian drew a short, quick breath. The many ways of saying no she couldn't fanned through her mind like pages in a book. Not one of them came into focus or conviction. Her excuses held no hope of any lasting happiness. Her palms were sweaty on the leather reins, her breath shallow and quick.

"Life's a card game, Jillian. You can't win by just watching. Take the card. Don't say anything now. I swear, if you said 'no' now, I'd sooner run off and live as a hermit. Think on it tonight. I'll find a way to come by the hospital tomorrow, and you can tell me then. Until then, we've a short ride up this hill, so let's pass the time as if we've not a care."

Jack smiled, relieved to know all his cards were on the table now. Instinctively, he knew better than to put any pressure on her to decide right away. She was an intelligent woman, and he recognized that she would make her choice without any more urging from him. He would abide by it, no matter what.

He settled back in his seat, put both his feet up on the footboard, his elbows on the seat back, and they bounced along with the swaying wagon.

Jillian stared straight ahead, unable to formulate a single sentence with the word "no" in it. —at least, not one she could bring herself to say. She swayed with the thumping wagon wheels, too. Or was that her heart?

She decided to take his advice and make small talk while they climbed the hill.

"So, what did you do, Jack, before you found your way up here in the mountains?"

Jack relaxed a bit more, seeing that she was following his lead. Like being dealt a high card, it was a good sign that a winning hand was near.

"Oh, I mined a lot growing up. Like my da. I started when I was sixteen. I heard the wages were better in America, so about four years ago I saved up and worked my way over on a steamship. When I got to New York—oh, that's a hard town when you're just off the boat—I took any job I could find just to live. Then I went to Pennsylvania when I heard it was a lot like the mines in Ireland. Too similar, though: coal. So I got out and headed west.

"By train to Chicago. That's where I started makin' more money playin' cards than a real job. I did regular work, too, but I started to notice luck was gettin' real friendly.

"When I got to Colorado, I found a spot at a gold mine. The Independence, it's called. It sure was different from coal mining."

It was his first experience around gold and all the trouble it could bring. Gold glistened in the eyes of the men who worked there, and Jack saw the disease that drove some men to greed—and sometimes death at its hand.

Jack laughed softly, still protecting his sore ribs.

"They had their own lawmen. The Pinkertons handled the heavy stuff, like guarding shipments, but the company had other gun men, some of them one step ahead of the law themselves. I was heading home from a card game one night when one of those 'company men,' name of Pike—I'd seen him around before—he tried to waylay me. I guess he knew about the game, and he stopped me in an alley, asking if I was someone named Johnson. Something told me he wasn't on the level, and when he tried to lay his hands on me, I gave him a good poke and lit out."

A voice in his head that night told Jack it was a ruse to trump up a reason to haul Jack to "jail" and take his card money. Pike lunged to grab him, but Jack landed a vicious blow to Pike's nose, and he fell to the ground, unconscious. Jack was quicker on his feet than the drunks Pike normally encountered, and he managed to escape into an alley and over a wooden fence into the darkness.

Believing he may have killed the company man, Jack decided to make a quick departure from the city and try his luck in Montana, where he had heard opportunities were plentiful. He worked various jobs at several mines, so that he was able to handle just about anything that needed filling—carpenter, mucker, pipefitter, trackman, sawyer. All were jobs that he held at one time or another, some briefly but usually satisfyingly to the bosses.

In his travels across the country, he was always able to find the right job at the right time, and he eventually moved on to a place whose name he had picked up along the way: Granite. It was said to have everything a man could want: work, lodging, food, and, of course, saloons and cards. So, by foot, coach, and rail, Jack made his way to the city on the mountainside.

At one point in the ride, he even told Jillian about The Green Isle and how he planned to be his own boss someday.

"Haven't you had enough trouble with saloons and gambling, Jack?" she asked.

"Oh, but this will be a high-class place. No riff-raff allowed. I know a good saloon from a bad one."

He left the details for their coming train ride, but he left no doubt that his financial future looked bright.

"So there you have it. Here I am. Luckier than I hoped I'd be."

"Lucky?" said Jillian. "I think you're still addled. Unless being robbed and beaten is lucky."

"And I'd take that beatin' again if it put me in this wagon."

She had no answer to that, and again Jack took note.

23

THE SILVER AND OTHER VALUABLES THAT CAME out of the ground at Granite did not arrive in the sunlight all shiny and ready to be minted into new quarters and dimes and dollars. The rock ore had to be crushed into a fine consistency so it could be processed and smelted into ingots and shipped back east to add to the investors' wealth.

The first step in turning rocks into U.S. dollars was to crush them into fine sand in a stamp mill. The stamp was an iron weight lifted and dropped repeatedly by way of rotating cams on a horizontal shaft. The common design was for multiple stamps to be operated in a line.

Now imagine the noise created by such a contraption. Just below the main shaft at Granite, the company had built two such mills—imaginatively named Mills A and B—containing a combined seventy stamps. The sound of the continuously falling stamps rumbled on twenty-four hours a day and could not only be heard but also felt through the ground in the vicinity of the mills.

That night, as Jillian lay in bed trying to fall asleep, she was used to feeling the gentle thrumming of the stamp mills less than a quarter mile away, up the mountainside. During the day, it was imperceptible, but at night, when everything was still, the sound carried far. She could sense the distant rumble at the very edge of hearing—like a giant, prehistoric purring cat from a fairy tale.

But now, they no longer ran all night long. When they stopped, the silence itself was enough to keep her awake, as were her reflections on a life that wasn't what she expected.

Growing up in Philipsburg, Jillian understood that being married was considered "normal," and as a little girl, she naturally assumed that would be her future as well. She was well-educated and considered herself well-read. The literature that she was exposed to provided the same examples of normality. She knew it was only a matter of time until she, too, would find her place as a wife.

When she turned twenty, she took a position as a nurse at the company hospital up in Granite and was immediately popular among patients and staff alike. She was competent, organized, and—most importantly—not squeamish. Mining injuries were violent and bloody. If a life could be saved at all, it took fast work and cooperation between the attending physician and his nurse.

But soon after she started work there, some of the working men found reason to come to the hospital for treatment of some imagined malady, just to meet the new nurse. She was smart enough, even then, to maintain a respectable demeanor and not be lured into questionable conversation.

The doctor in charge at that time, Dr. Horace Thane, a much older man and a very capable doctor, became a kind of father figure to her, and preemptively counseled her against letting herself be enamored by the rough miners who seemed to come drifting around more frequently.

He cautioned her, "Miss McCain, you are certainly competent as a nurse, and I'm glad to have you in the hospital's employ. But I must caution you against letting yourself be swept away by these tough men. You're a young lady, and no doubt flattered by so many admirers, but be circumspect in your allowances. Most of them do not have your best interests at heart, only their own."

She took the doctor's advice to heart and comported herself with professional remoteness—even coolness—to keep the men at bay. Eventually, the epidemic of hypochondria petered out.

Jillian learned a lot from the kind doctor, mostly on the job or from medical texts Thane loaned her. Thane was as good a teacher as he was a doctor; patient and instructive. He seemed to enjoy demonstrating what she needed to know and do, many things a doctor wouldn't be expected to perform.

He was somewhat large in the middle and loved a good meal. He was a widower, having lost his wife to cancer many years earlier, and Jillian would occasionally prepare him a home-cooked meal.

He and Jillian had a fine working relationship—as equals, or as equal as nineteenth-century mores would allow.

Then, one hot July afternoon, after walking all the way from the hoist house back to the hospital, Doctor Thane suffered a massive heart attack and passed dead away in the hospital kitchen, where he often poked about in search of sweets.

His replacement was a young and handsome Robert Brandt, not quite young at ten years her senior, but he commanded much local respect as the town warmed to him.

Soon after assuming his role, he and Jillian realized it was pointless to go on denying the feelings that had grown between them, working together every day. She was young, intelligent, highly gifted as a nurse, and not hesitant to act in her duties. He recognized the strength in her, and she in him. Their gifts and talents helped them work as a team. She looked up to his strong, sometimes forceful will, and assumed that if she held up her end of the work in a marriage, everything would be fine.

He occasionally alluded to having been through some hardships in his Army days, but never talked in detail about his experiences. She only imagined the horrible things he had seen and forgave him his occasional temper.

Any man would have had effects from such things, but in recent months, his anger would flare for no reason she could imagine. More often now it was aimed at her—again, for no discernible cause— and she felt less and less inclined to forgive his outbursts.

Meeting Jack Fallon might have been the luckiest event in her life if she could find the courage to embrace what he had proposed. She stayed busy in her duties, but in the few minutes she had to herself during the working day, thoughts of another life had begun to take root.

In her years of administering to the sick and injured miners and men of the town, she had never once felt anything more than professional compassion for her patients. But ever since that first glimmer in Jack's one swollen eye that first day, she sensed something different in the way she felt each time she tended to him. For the longest time it was indeed professional, and then it became more familiar, like friends passing time together. Then those moments became something to look forward to in her day. Now, whenever they met, she felt much more, deep within. When she imagined his arms around her, she could feel her pulse quicken and knew it was pointless to deny it any longer. This was the love she had waited for all her life. It saddened her to feel locked into a meaningless marriage.

Do I really deserve to live on like this? Or do I dare take the risk of stepping into the unknown with a stranger?

However she rephrased the same questions, the same answers prevailed. The steady rumbling from the stamp mills on the hillside above eventually helped her drift into a restless sleep, and the tossed coin ultimately landed heads-up.

24

TWO DAYS LATER, JACK WAS STILL ON LIMITED work around the office when Mr. Kelley assigned him to take a wagonload of crated company records down to the train station in Philipsburg. As part of the shutdown, a lot of files and freight would be shipped back to St. Louis or elsewhere, where some of the equipment could be used in the company's other interests. It was good to get out and actually do something useful. He felt he was recovered enough to assume his normal work, but for some reason, Kelley kept finding busy work for him to do. Not looking a gift horse in the mouth, Jack headed to the woodcutters' shop to find the wagon.

True to his word, a short time later, Jack pulled the wagon up to Han Liu's laundry just as Han walked out.

"Mister Jack! You come to visit. All good now?"

"Hello, Han," said Jack. "Yes, I'm good now. How are you? And you can call me Jack. No 'Mister' is necessary. I work for a living just like you."

"Okay, Jack, I will."

"What do you say, Han? Need a ride to town?"

Han grinned, "You just in time, Jack. I go to see uncle in town for laundry things. Paper, twine, things."

"Ha! I knew it! That's why I whistled up this horse for ya."

Jack pointed to the bench seat of the wagon, and Han climbed up. They headed off like they owned the road and were soon rumbling downhill toward town.

Jack was still new at driving a horse and wagon, and many times he struggled to keep their speed under control down the mountain. But he enjoyed the challenge and the freedom. He dismissed immediately the notion of taking the wagon to make his getaway with Jillian. Thievery was not in his nature, and besides, he didn't need to add larceny to his sins.

When their conversation faded, Jack saw his opening.

"Han, I've a confession to make, but you've got to promise you won't tell anyone. Can you do that?"

"Jack, we are good friends. If you say 'Han, don't tell,' Han does not tell." He chuckled, "Besides, who will I tell? Nobody pay attention Han."

"Well, you know Jillian Brandt at the hospital?"

"Oh, yes, Miss Jillian. Very nice lady."

"You know she's married to the good doctor?"

Han grew quiet, and the smile left his face. He looked away and said quietly, "Married, yes. Not sure if it's good. Doctor, sometimes not too nice."

"I agree on that score. Listen, with the mine closing…" Jack paused. It took all his nerve to speak the words aloud. "Jillian and I have decided to run away."

Han just looked at him in surprise. After considering it for a few moments, he nodded.

"I think she should. Yes. It cannot be good with him sometimes."

"You've no idea. But look, here's what's up. We're going to get on the train. I'll stay in Philipsburg that night before so I can meet her at the station the next morning. I'm telling you all this because, well, things will get complicated, and I want you to know I've appreciated our friendship."

"I understand, Jack. Me, too."

"But you're the only one who knows, and you're a good friend. I feel like I owe you an explanation—like I shouldn't just disappear and leave you wondering what happened."

Han didn't really know how to respond to that, but then he brightened.

"Hey—You need a place to stay that night before. When we go to uncle's house, I will ask him."

"Oh, no, Han. That's not necessary. I'll find a place somewhere."

"Jack, I know when things are hard. Mine closes. Job ends. Now with Miss Jillian, you have hard road coming. Uncle Thomas will help. Please let me help you, too."

Jack relented. One more detail tidied up.

In Philipsburg, they pulled into the lot where Han's uncle had his laundry business. It was just off Broadway on the hill coming down from Granite. Jack and Jillian had driven past it last week, and he never noticed it was there. At the time, it wasn't important, but now it was the perfect place to rest up and perhaps keep watch for Jillian the next morning.

Han introduced his uncle, Tom Yen, whose English was almost as good as Han's. Whenever Jack ran into Chinese who spoke English better than some of his friends, it reminded him not to judge people by their looks. He agreed at once to let Jack stay overnight. He showed them to a room off the cellar that would do fine. It had a simple cot and side table, but the rest of the space was taken up by shelves of food, musty winter clothes, and chemicals for the laundry.

Jack was unsure when he might arrive, but Tom showed him how to come in if it was late at night or if no one was home. Jack offered, but Tom refused any payment.

"Friend of Han," he said. "Not to pay. Don't think of it."

Jack shook his hand and helped Han load the few things he had come for into the wagon. They said goodbye and headed off to the train station to finish Jack's assignment.

He was glad Han had come along, as the two of them made short work of unloading their cargo. Jack gave Kelley's shipping instructions to the station manager, and they returned to Granite.

When they got back to Han's shop, Jack helped him unload again, and they went their separate ways.

"Remember, Han. Our secret, right?"

"Han don't know what you talk about, Jack," said Han, grinning as he disappeared into the shop.

25

THE SATURDAY BEFORE THE MINE WAS TO BE closed for good, the union bosses called a meeting to inform their members of the somewhat limited future of the company. The second-floor meeting hall at Granite Miner's Union Hall filled beyond capacity with over 200 men. Because it was in the heat of August, the meeting was held after supper. By then, most of the men had nearly exhausted the last shipment of beer—perhaps forever from the brewery down in Philipsburg.

All the windows were open, and the heat of the day was slowly draining out of the room. Those who couldn't find space, or who came a bit late, gathered on the street outside. As usual, the Finns and Swedes all sat off to one side. Most had limited understanding of English, and the few who did acted as informal interpreters, repeating in hushed voices what was said up on the stage. The same was true of the Italians on the opposite side. Small knots of other languages formed around the room.

Jack and Tim were surrounded by their shift mates toward the back of the hall, but Jack knew what was coming.

He hadn't repeated the contents of the telegram to anyone, but rumors had flown through town like a banshee. His plans with Jillian, whether they came true or not, depended on the details he would learn tonight. How the company would scale down the closure, what work might be left to do, and most importantly, when he could count on being free of his work obligations so he could, hopefully, escape with her.

Jimmy Gilfillen called the meeting to order, and it took many minutes for the jostling and grumbling to cease. He finally resorted to banging his gavel on the podium and calling for quiet a second time, then a third, before reasonable silence took over.

"Now I want everyone to remember, we're all on the same side here. No one is getting over on anyone else. I'm here to tell this membership—"

"Is the mine closing, Jimmy?" shouted Hans Bergmann from the center of the crowd.

"Yeah, are we quit?" said another man.

"Will it close down?" repeated several others around the crowded room. The question, in various forms, echoed around the room at levels of volume and anger.

Gilfillen banged his gavel until everyone quieted down again. He paused until he knew all were listening. He decided there was no way to ease into it.

"Yes. The mine will close."

There was a general release of epithets and shouting. The roaring crowd echoed from one end of Broadway to the other. This time, Jimmy let it burn itself out before he continued.

"I have been informed by the mine superintendent, Mr. Weir, that because silver prices have dropped recently due to politics in Washington, this mine—and many others, I'll add—are shutting down. The mine companies simply don't have the profits to continue for the time being."

The room erupted again with shouting and stomping, mostly aimed at their St. Louis headquarters, but a few more informed members blamed the "idiots in Washington," as Kelley had called them weeks ago. Some of the foreign-born miners questioned their decision to come to the New World.

When another lull occurred, Jimmy went on. "Now, both Mr. Weir and Mr. Kelley have assured me that they intend to keep as many men working for as long as they can, but, as you've seen lately, they're under orders from St. Louis to cut jobs and shifts."

He raised his hands as the crowd noise grew again.

"I know, I know. Some men have already left voluntarily, and we're all sad to see them off, but I'm afraid it's coming down to much more than that. On Monday, there will only be one shift active. The men from second and third shift, well, show up at the company office, and you'll be told if there's work for you, and for how long."

Tim leaned close to Jack's shoulder. "This is bad. I've been here two years, and now it's 'so long and good luck'?"

Jack said nothing. He never counted his winnings at cards while he was still at the game, but now he mentally added up his savings at the company bank and what his final debts might be at the boarding house and the company store. His story at Granite was about to end, and in his heart, he was eager to close that book. And start the next one.

At the announcement of Monday's single shift, the noise in the Union Hall grew even louder. It wasn't a dance or a wedding. It was a funeral. For the whole town.

Gilfillen continued, "I'm told it will probably go by seniority. Those who've been with the company the longest will be the last to be let go. You can figure that out among yourselves. I'm sorry, lads, but there it is. I've assured the management that this union isn't going to strike or take retribution against the company. What would be the point? If they do reopen in the future, who wants to taint their record by being a troublemaker? Again, I'm sorry, men. But let's give them a decent shutdown, and we'll collect our wages as honest men. This union has locals in other towns, and anyone who signs on with one of those outfits is welcome to keep up his membership."

"Keep paying his dues, you mean!" someone shouted from the back.

There was general laughter around the room, but Jimmy just nodded. *Well, at least they're not going to lynch the bosses or tear the building down.*

There being no further business of any interest to the membership, the meeting was adjourned. The barkeepers did what they could to save some of the vanishing beer for later in the week, hoping they could negotiate at least one more order from Silver Spray Brewery down in the valley. They at least didn't raise the price of the dwindling supply of cold beer that night.

But after the meeting, most of the men were not in a festive mood. Once the conversation died down after the gavel fell, virtually all of them filed out and headed home, either alone or to deliver the news to their families that they were soon to be unemployed.

Ticking off the things he needed to do without delay, Jack resolved to visit the bank when it opened and clean out his money. It would be safely hidden in his room until he was prepared to leave town. He'd settle up with Buskett Mercantile, the company store, for the few work things he'd purchased on credit. And pay his rent at Mrs. Headley's. Then he would make one last visit to Han's laundry, wishing they had enjoyed more rides together. Of course, everything revolved around Jillian's answer to his—what was it? Certainly not a proposal, not in *that* sense. His suggestion. His question, at least. He hoped she made the right choice.

Jack and Tim, and a few others, spied McFeeney on his way down the stairs to the street. Tim called out to him as they hit the street and caught up to him.

"Hey, Mac!" Tim poked him in the chest. "Mac, don't tell me you didn't know this was coming."

"Now, Kearney, listen to me. I'm in and out of the company office ten times a day. I don't—"

Tim grabbed his lapel, but Jack put his hand on Tim's arm. He released him.

"Boys, this isn't Mac's fault," Jack said. "What good would it do even if he had known? If any of us knew? Do you think he could talk them out of closing?"

They turned down Broadway. It was unspoken, but their destination, as always, was Rosemary's saloon. Thirsty or not, they understood their nights together at the bar were numbered. Best to enjoy each other's company while they could.

Outwardly, Jack acted as normally as he could, laughing with his friends as they all put on a strong face with the end of their jobs in sight. They even played a few last rounds of cards, though no one made bets or kept score.

But inside, he could only think of Jillian. Until now, he had only himself to worry about. Everything else in his life was organized and ready to adapt to the uncertainty of searching for work, finding work, losing work, and searching again. The sensation of having to account for the needs of someone else in his plans was something new entirely. It felt good.

26

WHEN THE SHIFT WHISTLE BLEW AT THE MINE ON
Monday, Jack had finally been put back to real work and was
at his usual place in line waiting to ride the cage down the
shaft. The conversation among the men was all about the
mine closing and their jobs disappearing like smoke on the
wind. Jack held up his end of the grumbling, but it was as if
two separate conversations were taking place in his head, for
his mind was on what Jillian's answer would be.

That he was in love with her was finally a fact he admitted, if only to himself. When the proper time came, he
would admit it to her, too.

*I just hope I don't have to say it as if I'm begging her to leave
with me.*

All of it went round and round in his head. Rough men
don't speak of such things to each other, and besides, there
was no one with whom Jack could share his hopes and
plans. Tim Kearney was the closest he had to a best friend,
but even he would never accept or understand the totality of
the circumstances surrounding Jillian and her sad marriage.

But the logical part of his brain was busily laying plans for two possibilities.

One: the good and proper Mrs. Brandt would insist that he not have any further contact with her; that she would rather suffer in silence than endure the ridicule and embarrassment of leaving a husband the whole town respected and looked to for aid and comfort in sickness and injury.

Perfectly understandable. Also perfectly wrong. But Jack was man enough to take "no" for an answer, and he would pack his sorrows in his kit and head down the mountain alone.

And alone he would remain. No one else could ever bring forth the dizzy feeling he felt in the pit of his stomach whenever she came into view. He knew that for a fact, just as he knew which end of a shovel to hold onto.

Or, two: she would say "yes," in which case he would need a plan ready to have a head start, so that no one could find them. His greatest hope was that, if she decided to go, it would mean that she might have feelings for him in return, or at least be willing to let them grow in time.

The possible outcomes kept Jack's mind awhirl as the mine cage lowered him and his crewmates down the shaft. He plodded through his shift, trying to concentrate on the physical work at hand, while trying not to let his attention wander so much that he became another casualty of mining just when his life might change so drastically for the better. The dialogue in his head was so animated at times that he felt surely someone nearby would overhear and think he was mad.

The trick will be to find a way for her to go to the train station at the proper time. Idiot: The trick will be to convince her to go at all.

On and on it went, through one ore cart after another. Through lunch. Through hauling drill hoses up from the last working drift, nearly losing his foot to a runaway ore cart barreling down the tracks in the tunnel—a not-uncommon injury. Although now the carts were carrying tools and equipment, the ore no longer needed.

By the end of his shift, Jack believed he had every angle thought out and all contingencies accounted for. The hardest question: would she go?

One thing he refused to consider was trying to talk her into it. He only wanted to offer her a way to a real life. If that life was with him, then so much the better.

Finally, the shift whistle sounded, and men began making their way up to the surface. None of his shift mates seemed to notice his distraction.

"Union Hall tonight, Jack?" Alan asked. "We're having billiards. Might be our last game."

"I'm no good with that stick, Alan. The only stick and balls I enjoy watching are the lads at the ball field," Jack said.

"Just a pint, then?"

"Maybe."

The cage started up to the surface, and Alan leaned closer. "You worry me, Jack boy. You're so serious lately. Is your head still a-hurtin'?"

"Serious enough for this place," Kearney joined in, laughing. "It's enough to dull the brain."

They all laughed at that.

Jack's laugh was forced. It wasn't in his eyes.

"There's dark clouds ahead, boys," Jack said. "Don't forget, we're all about to be on the road."

The cage reached the top of the shaft, and they all tagged out for the day, hanging their numbered metal tabs on the board in the hoist room.

A few more shifts and Jack and the rest would hang their tags for the last time.

Before leaving for their homes, they visited The Dry. The ones who had worked other mines would miss the luxury of a place like this to wash up at the mine workings. After a wash and a change, the shift of miners drifted apart down the road.

As they went their separate ways, Jack and Tim were left walking together. Jack was quiet, thinking about how he used to roam from job to job. Jillian gave meaning to his ramblings, and he was anxious to start this next journey.

"Jack, don't listen to Alan and the rest of them," Tim said. "I can see you're worried. You've got trouble, eh?"

"Nah, Tim, I'm just—"

Tim grabbed his elbow.

"This is me, boy-o. And if I had to guess, I'd bet all the money in my pocket against all the money in your pocket that it's a woman who's got you walkin' on a rail."

Jack took a deep breath. "Tim, you're a good friend and I'm glad of it. But we've only a few more days of work in this town, and what's in my head will stay in my head. Really. I'm better off figuring things out on my own."

Tim chewed his lower lip. "If you say so. But when there's machinery involved, just know I'll be watchin' over you like a guardian angel." He grinned and nudged Jack hard with his elbow. "Until your real angel can take over the job."

His head was brimming with ideas: how to arrange an innocent encounter with Jillian, how to find out the train schedule, which would take most of a day if he walked the four miles to Philipsburg and back.

Then it came to him. The Metropolitan Hotel was a popular spot for visitors that had a famous restaurant where people enjoyed the best dinner in town, probably even in the state. Maybe they had train schedules posted in the lobby. He passed the spot where he had lain unconscious that cold night he was robbed, and where Han had found him the next morning. There had been no word from the sheriff on the hunt for the two gamblers, and Jack grudgingly accepted the fact that his troubles on that score would see no closure. Of the many fond memories he would take with him when leaving Granite, that was not one of them.

Except, of course, that it brought him and Jillian together. Whether that memory remained in the "fond" column—or was best forgotten—would be decided soon.

27

"I'M SORRY IT'S COME TO THIS." THOMAS WEIR leaned back in his chair. Robert Brandt stood in front of Weir's desk in the company office, an uneasy feeling growing inside him. "But I don't control the purse strings. Closing the mine is up to the investors in St. Louis, and it's their money. In my opinion, it's also their own throats they're cutting by pulling out of this mine."

Doctor Brandt had thought the meeting would be about his recent request for more medical supplies and equipment for the hospital. Of course, he had heard the rumors around town that the mine might reduce operations or even close for a while until things calmed down. But he had dismissed the talk out of hand—some people revel in causing fears. Now the whole company was folding up? He had just learned he would soon be unemployed.

When he left the Army and settled into the life of a doctor for the mining company, he believed it was all he wanted in life: not being forced to move from place to place, to order his own life the way he saw fit, with no one to question him or doubt his abilities and authority. It just wasn't fair. This company didn't understand what it took to provide real medical care in this frontier town, so far from real civilization. He had done more than his share of miracles with the meager tools and supplies that St. Louis would provide. Didn't anyone realize his talents?

"What about the town?" Dr. Brandt asked. "Thousands of people depend on the mine, and the miners' money that's spent here. If the mine closes, the town will vanish. The hospital will close…"

"I understand, Robert, and you've done well here as our physician. The Granite Hospital is a first-rate institution. You've helped a lot of people. Delivered more than a few babies. I'm happy to give you a letter of recommendation for wherever you choose to go. There's no need to be in a hurry, though. As I said, the mine will cease operating on Friday, but I'm sure people will still need your services for many days or weeks thereafter."

Weir cleared his throat and took on an even sadder look.

"However, payment from the company will have to cease on Friday. Maybe you can work out some form of payment from your patients afterward."

He lowered his voice. "But if you get anything serious, just come see me and we'll figure out something. Again, I'm sorry."

"Well, thank you for letting me know personally, Mr. Weir," Dr. Brandt said. "I will make arrangements with some of my patients and… if you'll excuse me, then, I should get back and see to the hospital and, see to its…"—he swallowed hard—"closing."

"Of course. If you need help with anything, manpower or whatnot, don't hesitate to ask. Good day, Robert."

Brandt walked back to the hospital, downhill from the company office, as if in a trance. He spoke to no one on the busy street and could only think of what the future could hold. *What future?* His life would be turned upside down. There wouldn't be enough income from the few people who remained in town to support him and Jillian. A broken bone here and there. A birth now and then, if any young people even decided to stay on. Which was doubtful, as they would have to go where the work was, too.

As he reached for the side entrance to the hospital, he noticed that his fists were clenched as though he was preparing for a brawl. The stress of being uprooted was building inside him, and he took a few deep breaths before entering. Telling Jillian they would soon have to pick up and move to someplace new was not a conversation he looked forward to. He could almost hear her voice, searching for any excuse to delay a move so she might spend more time with that miner. He was sure that slacker had malingered his way through several weeks of convalescence in Brandt's hospital just to be near his wife.

In all the years they had lived and worked around these strapping young mining boys, she had never strayed. He was dead certain of that. It was only lately that it had become obvious that there was some kind of infatuation growing with this Fallon fellow. If she made one utterance about procrastinating their departure, Brandt would force her to admit what was going on. He'd deal with it head-on and be done with it forever.

I will not be embarrassed and humiliated by having a wandering wife. This city can lose its only doctor and burn to the ground before I let that Fallon get away with ruining my reputation.

But in the back of his mind, another idea began to form—something to keep in his pocket just in case things got out of hand. He refused to let the thought grow to fruition, because to do so would mean he might succumb to a long-dead darkness—one he had vanquished years ago when he still wore the uniform of the United States. When the enemy died in the thousands at the hands of a modern military. And, for mortally wounded patients, at his own hand, when death took a shortcut.

As a doctor on the frontier, he had treated all the major wounds of battle—gunshot, artillery, arrows, trampled by horses—and all the diseases of encampment and fort life, from dysentery to syphilis to cholera.

Brandt had come upon the remnants of atrocities after several battles and was horrified by the sight. Such brutality could do long-term damage to a 19th-century mind.

He made no excuses for what he felt after his service. Though it often weighed on his heart, what service could he offer to a dying man with no scalp, or arms or legs, begging for merciless relief? A bullet was the quickest medication, and he believed he was being humane.

But a doctor's not supposed to kill, he often cried inside.

But kill he did, when no other quick ending was possible. In the few instances when anyone else was present, no one questioned his decision. They knew as well that there was nothing to be done. It was always a last resort, of course, many times at the patient's own urging if he was conscious. He had also come upon cases where a man's friends had dispatched him quickly to relieve his suffering long before the doctor could arrive on the field.

Over time, his revulsion at this detestable final act dissipated, and killing became… not quite easier, but bearable.

The mental torment went on, even years later, deep inside. It frightened him to imagine what he might be capable of if the circumstances were repeated. But what if they weren't repeated? Or were not similar at all? The first killing was as sinful as the seventh or eighth.

Now the enemy was here, in ones and twos, and Brandt refused to be on the losing side.

By the time he entered the hospital, Robert's mood had turned dark, with an undercurrent of desperation about what his future held. They would be leaving soon, surely. What kind of life would they have if she had a wandering heart? Even in a new town with Fallon far behind her, how could he trust her not to stray?

To distract from his worries, he began doing what he always did: making decisions, taking a course of action. Right or wrong, time would tell. But he always acted promptly when circumstances called for it. He was the man in charge, after all. He was The Doctor.

He could arrange to have their household goods packed and shipped to whatever destination he chose. His account at the Freychlag Bank in town had enough to see them through for a while. His finances were now in jeopardy, and he took greater care to make them last.

Robert sat down at the desk in his office to plan their inevitable departure.

28

THE PROPRIETORS OF THE BUSY SHOPS AND BUSI-
nesses along Granite's main street had no official notice of
the looming mine closure. Oh, there had been rumors every
few years, and the smarter ones always knew mining towns
come and go at the drop of a hat or the dwindling of a rich
vein of ore. But as Jillian made her way from shop to shop,
gathering a few days' worth of groceries, she felt the owners were acting as if business was normal and would go on
forever.

The smarter businessmen, however, knew how to read a
ledger and could see their shops slipping into failure—slowly at first, but unmistakably faster now. As they were able,
they paid off their debts, and one by one, they began closing
up. Some moved down to Philipsburg, where mines plucked
metals other than silver out of the ground. Others gave up
entirely and left the area. Even the shop where she bought
fresh fruit had been shuttered, and she had to search for
Robert's apples elsewhere.

It seemed the harder she tried, she could not drive out
the impossible visions of a life elsewhere. When a person is

held under water for so long, she either drowns or finds an escape. The things she read in books weren't only fantasy—they could reflect true life, given the proper incentive.

Then she would rein it all in and try to convince herself that she was already living the life she had been dealt. Like a bad hand of cards—

That was something Jack would say—cards. And again, she was off on another mental tangent.

To look at the thing logically, she reasoned, *you have to plan for alternatives, designs, and all kinds of details.*

The two of them staying in Granite was not an option by any means. There would be all kinds of gossip—all of it bad. Neither of them would have much chance of finding employment with the stigma—one of them a home-wrecker, the other from a failed marriage—hanging over them. Besides, Granite itself might be on the wane.

There was a regular train in Philipsburg that ran to Drummond and made connections there for other trains, or even overland coach. It depended on how fast—or how discreetly—they wanted to get far, far away.

Then there was the matter of her things. She had accumulated many possessions, more than would fit in a simple valise. She doubted they could manage a steamer trunk if they had to travel far and fast. She began thinking of essentials that she could fit into a suitcase.

But not to pack just yet. What would Robert do if he discovered a packed bag? He would, of course, ask unanswerable questions. She shivered in the warm sun, walking back to the hospital with her basket.

She was putting things away in the kitchen, her mind far off, when Robert walked in.

"I had a meeting with the mine boss today," he said.

She startled and nearly dropped a can.

"What's wrong? You jumped just now?"

"You startled me, that's all. I thought you were out."

"Sorry," he taunted her, "I'm not your miner boy come snooping around."

Jillian caught herself before snapping back. She remembered clearly what happened the last several times she denied his accusations. So she pursed her lips and changed the subject.

"What was your meeting about?"

"The mine is closing."

"We've heard those rumors before." She turned to face him and leaned back against the counter. "For sure this time? What will that mean?"

"It means I'm out of work. Or will be soon enough. I'm considering our next move. Butte, probably. There are many more mines there, and I should be able to find a position."

For Jillian, what had been only a mental exercise was quickly approaching reality. The leisurely accumulation of possibilities started running together. If they were going to be moving, she would be packing a bag at some point—not so suspicious in itself now. There might even be talk of train schedules or travel routes that she would pay close attention to for her own purposes.

Jillian never considered herself a schemer, but now there were two people in her life who would be trying to lead her in one direction or another. Best to be prepared and have answers either way.

"Butte is a much bigger place, I hear," she said. "You should have no trouble finding a place there. Maybe even another hospital."

"We, my dear…" He seemed to be forcing his nicety. "*We* surely will find a place there."

He walked to the window and parted the curtains, watching the slow traffic on the Philipsburg Road.

"This mine closure is probably a good thing," he said. "You need to get away from this little town. These miners are too needy. Butte has a higher class of people."

She knew he was trying to goad her, but she refused to play into his hands.

"And our things? We'll need a bigger wagon than we have now."

Robert stepped closer to her and reached to take an apple from the bowl on the counter behind her. She knew he was again trying to get a reaction from her, but she didn't flinch at his closeness.

"I've considered that," he said. "We'll travel light. Just our carriage and a few bags. I'll arrange to have our property shipped. Otherwise, we'd be waiting too long, wasting time. There will be plenty of men available to do some packing for us at a reasonable expense very soon."

Of course, he meant out-of-work miners willing to do anything for a few dollars. He was not above taking advantage of others in desperate straits.

Brandt gave up tempting her into an argument. He could see she was amenable to whatever he would suggest just now. The time to really watch her would be closer to their leaving, when she might try to see that "miner boy" again to say goodbye. If that happened—he caught himself—his temper almost flared again. He could feel the physical effects from a detached, clinical perspective: quickening heartbeat, flushed face, shorter respiration, maxillofacial muscles tensing. He took a few deep breaths and smiled at Jillian, but not with his eyes.

"We'll leave early next week. It'll be fine."

She nodded and smiled also. And began to plan.

29

THE PLAN IN JACK'S MIND WAS REPEATEDLY COM-
ing together, then falling apart as he imagined all sorts of
likely directions and complications. Eventually, he decided
on a course of action that stood the best chance, though
none were perfect.

They should not be seen together if at all possible. Their
stroll down Main Street the day he carried her groceries
probably garnered enough attention around town to wend
its way back to the doctor's ears by now. The longer he could
avoid someone noticing the two of them together again, the
better.

Once they left, word would surely get to Brandt, and
he would come racing down the mountain looking for his
wife—and for Jack, with non-healing intent. Jack was determined to avoid anyone who might tell the doctor that his
errant wife was traveling in the company of a miner.

But there was no evading the eventual sight of the two
of them boarding the northbound train. With so many people departing lately, they might blend in with the crowd—
except that the crowd would no doubt consist of friends and

neighbors. They would have to board separately and reunite in Drummond to find another train westward.

As Jack firmed up his plans, he found that the train schedule was indeed posted in the lobby of the Metropolitan Hotel. The daily train left Philipsburg at noon, so they would need to be close to the station by then. An early morning ride down from Granite should put them comfortably in place, with time to buy tickets and board two different rail cars.

The hardest part would be for Jillian to find a reason to ride down early in the morning, either with or without the doctor knowing. But the plan was all for nothing if he couldn't tell her about it.

On Tuesday after his shift, Jack loitered around the streets near the hospital, hoping Jillian might appear. His patience paid off. She rounded the corner onto Main Street on her way to the butcher's shop.

Jack pretended to be walking with purpose in the opposite direction. Their eyes met while they were still some distance apart. Jack looked furtively around—there were a few people about—so he gave her a short shake of his head.

When they were only a few feet apart, Jillian stopped and pretended to search her purse for something, and Jack slowed as he passed.

"Meet me at the ball field," he said quietly. "No one goes there during the week."

They nodded in passing, as strangers do on the street, and went their separate ways.

Jack continued down Main Street and then further, down the Philipsburg Road, where the baseball field lay just outside of town. He walked completely around the open space, keeping to the shade of the trees. Most of the mountainside had been denuded for firewood to operate the steam boilers for the mines, and for heating homes and shops. But foresight had saved enough of them to shade spectators at the ballpark from the summer sun.

As she bought a few groceries, Jillian couldn't help but grow nervous about what they were contemplating. Her edginess had ebbed and flowed in recent days, but now it was like standing on a high roof, and the fluttering in her stomach grew with each breath.

What am I doing? Her voice shouted inside. *You're saving your own life, you silly goose. Draw the card.*

And with that, she ducked out the side door of the shop and headed uphill behind Main Street toward the ball field. She took a circuitous route, out of sight of passersby on the street. Especially out of view of the hospital, which faced the road leading down to Philipsburg.

When she arrived in the big open space, there was no one around. She could smell the grass in the sunshine and hear the breeze in the trees, but there was no sign of Jack or anyone else.

She walked the perimeter of the field, and on the side farthest away from the road, she spied him back in the shade.

"I thought you changed your mind," he said as she came closer.

"I can't believe I didn't."

"If you're doubting—"

She shook her head sharply. "No, no, it's not that. I'm sure, Jack."

They stood close enough to touch, but denied themselves the temptation. No one was in sight, but they instinctively knew that any physical surrender would be clearly visible on their faces for anyone to see.

Jack detailed the plan he had worked out. Separately, they had come to almost the same strategy.

They would purchase their train tickets at different times and board separate cars. Just knowing they would be in sight of each other gave them the courage to make the journey. Separately, but together.

Once they got to Drummond, he assured her, they would have smooth sailing. And, depending on whether anyone else from Granite was on the train, they might even sit together for the much longer ride westward.

"The way they're working us at the mine, shifts are running pretty late," said Jack. "But I'll be outside the hospital on Friday after I'm done work. Then we can go down and wait for the train somewhere out of sight. If you can't get away Friday night, I'll meet you at the station Saturday morning."

"I'll be ready."

There was nothing left to say. It all depended now on both of them being at the right place at the right time. He turned to leave, but Jillian touched his arm. All her dreams and wishes of recent weeks rose to the moment.

"Jack, remember when you offered to accompany me on the road, just for my safety? And then you'd say your goodbyes?"

Jack nodded, unaware he was holding his breath.

"I've decided. When we get to wherever it is we're going," she took a deep breath herself, "don't say goodbye. I mean, we deserve a chance to see the next card. Don't we?"

He let out a long breath and touched her cheek.

"That we do, Jillian. That we do."

When they parted, Jack lingered at the ball field so they didn't reappear in town at the same time. He felt uncomfortable that deception was becoming second nature, but it was vital to their success.

Jillian had no idea how she would find an excuse to make her getaway, but with each step, her courage grew. She was determined that—one way or another—she would be rid of Robert Brandt.

30

RECENT WORK DAYS HAD BEEN A JUMBLE. THE COM-
pany insisted they start on time, but it didn't seem to mind if
a shift ran many hours over. Since there was only one shift
per day, Jack and the last remaining underground crew had
been down in the pit gathering tools, drill bits, rock drills,
air pressure hoses, and all manner of equipment. The rock
drills were the biggest tools to be brought up, and took at
least two big men to carry each one back to the hoist elevators. There were also large water pumps on each level, but
management had decided much of it would be abandoned
to rust and rot, too much trouble and too time-consuming
to disassemble and bring up to the surface.

Jack was happy to leave as much equipment behind as
they wanted.

At the start of Jack's final shift at the mine, the shift boss,
Brownlow, addressed the crew as they gathered to make
their last descent. Those who hoped for a lighter workday
were disappointed to hear that, in the rush to clear out machinery over the past few weeks, several sections of tunnel in
the deepest part of the mine had been overlooked.

"I don't know how much is left at the bottom, but I want half of you men all the way down, and the other half to finish searching the levels from four hundred feet on up for anything useful."

There were groans all around. They knew how extensive the underground tunnels were. All drilling, blasting, and ore removal had ceased over a week ago, and they had been busy dismantling equipment and bringing it up ever since.

"As for the stuff at the bottom, the manager's inventory says there's more than we thought. So, find it, stage it at the lift station like you've been doing, and we'll get it up and done. Be careful at the bottom: the pumps were turned off last week, so you might see some water. Don't bother with flooded drifts. They knew they'd lose whatever's down there when they shut down the pumps. Just get what you can and we'll cross off the rest."

Brownlow was referring to the series of staging pumps that worked twenty-four hours a day to hold back the constant influx of water into the mine tunnels. Mud was a fact of life underground. Most of Jack's clothes had changed color from the constant soaking, drying, and scraping of mud. Han's laundry had quickly lost the ability to retain his working clothes' original color.

The shift boss tried to put the news that their last shift would run far longer than usual in a positive light. "Chin up, lads. The good news is our last day will fill our pockets."

Jack's mind quickly shifted to absorb the news. This last shift would run much later than the others. He wouldn't be able to meet Jillian tonight after all. But it would take the lift several trips, each round trip many minutes long, to get the whole crew down the shaft. He would not be missed for a while, so he slipped out of the hoist house unnoticed.

His first stop was at the laundry, but Han wasn't there. Nor could he make himself understood to Han's mother— or perhaps she was his grandmother; she looked old enough to be either—that he needed to find Han. He gave up and ran back up toward the hotels to look for him.

As luck would have it, they nearly bumped into each other at the corner of Broadway as Han came out of the Ruby Hotel with a load of laundry.

"Han!"

"Mister Jack! Hello to you, my friend."

Jack fell in beside Han as they headed back downhill toward the laundry.

"Han, remember when I told you I was leaving with Miss Jillian?" Jack said quietly.

"Yes. You go now?" Han half-whispered, picking up on Jack's discreet tone of voice.

"Maybe, Han, maybe. I need to get a message to her. The mine has closed—you know that, right?"

Han looked sad. "Yes, mother and father not know what to do now. Not work much for us now."

"I'm sorry, Han. I know you all work hard. Don't worry, you'll find a place. You should go soon, I think. Maybe open a new laundry down in Philipsburg. Otherwise, you'll be stuck up here on the mountain with no money."

"No money," said Han, with sadness in his voice at their uncertain future. Then he added thoughtfully, "Yes, cousins live down in town. We all can be alright."

As they reached the laundry, Jack held open the door, and they both entered. Han dumped the ball of laundry, all tied up in a bed sheet.

"You have message for Miss Jillian?"

"Right. We've been really busy closing up the mine workings, and our shifts are longer now. Jillian knows we're to meet at the train station down in town. But I might need her to—do you have something I can write on?"

Han ducked behind the counter of the shop and handed Jack a blank laundry ticket. It was plain white on the back, and he gave Jack a stubby pencil. It had to be short and meaningless to anyone else if it was intercepted.

Jack scribbled a few words and handed it back to Han.

"Just take this to her. And don't let anyone else see it, okay?"

"Okay, Jack. One note, one person, no one else. You betcha."

Jack put his hand on Han's shoulder. If things went as smoothly and as quickly as Jack hoped, they would probably never cross paths again.

"Thanks, Han. You know, I've only made a few friends on this mountain, and I'm glad you're one of them."

Jack held out his hand, and they shook, both knowing it was probably farewell. Han turned back to his laundry work, and Jack raced back up Broadway toward the mine yards.

31

AT ABOUT THE SAME TIME, JILLIAN WENT UP TO the second floor of the hospital to find Robert busily packing his valise in their bedroom. It was a big, well-worn leather and canvas satchel that was nearly the only thing he had saved from his Army days, except for his personal medical kit.

They had discussed their departure many times, but never with a firm date so she could begin her own packing. Something must have triggered his decision to leave sooner rather than later.

"Robert?" The rest of the question hung in the air.

"Yes. I've changed my mind, we're leaving," he said. "We've no patients right now, nor will we. None that could pay, anyway. The mine superintendent informed me that even if they sent us one, the company would no longer be willing to reimburse us for treatment. So we might as well go now while we can afford to."

"But I haven't packed anything. When are you planning—"

"We leave tonight."

"What?!"

"We'll stay down in Philipsburg tonight and take the morning train to Drummond. And from there, we'll head for Butte."

"But I… Robert, what about our household? We can't just leave everything we own behind. This is our lives."

"I've arranged to have it all packed and shipped. Don't worry. Just pack for a few nights until we get to Butte. We'll find a fine hotel there until we secure a permanent address." He looked around the room. "As permanent as this one was, I suppose."

Jillian realized it was useless to protest any further. Besides, this might be the confused situation she was hoping for.

"All right. I'll tell the orderly, Mr. Coates. Shall I settle our payment to the laundry boy, Han Liu? We can't leave unpaid debts."

Brandt thought for a moment and reasoned that if she stayed busy, she'd be less distracted by "that boy," as Robert always called him.

He began cinching up the straps on his bag.

"Fine. Take care of it. But be ready to leave by sundown. I don't like riding the carriage at night on that downhill road. But there's almost no one left on the road now anyway, so it should be safe enough." Then, more to himself, "This town will belong to the ghosts in a day or two."

Jillian went to the desk in Robert's office to find the outstanding balance owed to Han's family for their services. Then she drew the amount from a locked box in the bottom drawer and went downstairs. On her way out, she encountered Wallace Coates, and told him they were leaving. He was paid by the company, so they had no financial obligations to him. At least now he was free to find his own way.

Starting down toward Chinatown, she turned the situation over in her mind as she considered new possibilities. The plan might still work out. If she went down to Philipsburg tonight, pretending to be the dutiful wife, Robert might be less suspicious. She had to trust that Jack would find her, and they could board the train separately. Or, if she didn't see Jack at all at the station, she could find some excuse to be apart from Robert as the train started to pull out, then step off the train before it gained speed, somewhere that Robert wouldn't see her. She would find Jack and hide until the next day's train left, in case Robert returned looking for them. Or, better still, they could use the wagon to leave right away—to Butte, perhaps. Any direction opposite to what Robert planned.

———•

HAN HAD JUST RETURNED TO THE LAUNDRY WITH another load when Jillian hurried in, wearing the lightweight duster coat she intended to travel in later that night. She chose it for its long length and weather collar that she might have to turn up later against the chill of the night's ride.

She drew the envelope of cash from her purse. "Han, I've brought you the money for our cleaning bill this month. I'm sorry, we won't be needing your service anymore. It's been very good."

Han nodded, understanding their business was at an end. Han bowed slightly in acceptance.

"Thank you, Miss Jillian. Yes, everything is changing."

"Han, do you remember Jack Fallon? The man you—"

"Mister Jack, yes! Note from Mister Jack to you. Here, wait."

Han set the pile of laundry by the front counter, reached into his pocket, and handed her the slip.

"Here. Mister Jack said for you only. He said much work to do at the mine."

Jillian unfolded the scrap of paper and looked back at Han.

"Thank you, Han. This was good of you to do."

"Yes. I'm sorry, the mine is done." He shrugged, as if to say, *But that's life.*

Jillian stuffed the note in her coat pocket and went back to the hospital to pack a bag. Just for a few days, Robert had said.

She thought it could get complicated trying to separate herself from Robert and find Jack somewhere near the train station. But in the general confusion of so many people leaving town, there might be a chance.

Even if all they could do was make eye contact, at least they would know they were on the same train.

32

"WHERE DID YOU RUN OFF TO?" ASKED KEARNEY when Jack ducked back into the hoist room. The last group of men was just stepping into the cage when he caught up to them.

"I hate those thunderboxes down below," replied Jack, referring to the portable latrines.

Tim nodded in understanding, and they squeezed into the cage with the others.

On this last day of operation, the depth to which Jack's "bottom half" crew was assigned to work was at 1,550 feet. He, Tim Kearney, Red Clancy, and twelve other men made the trip down in three separate cages. It took about six minutes for each group to reach the lowest level. Then they split up and began searching through each level, collecting what machinery could be dismantled quickly and moving it to the lift.

The water pumps Brownlow had referred to were a series of lifting pumps at each level of the mine, meant to keep the tunnels from filling with water that seeped in naturally. There were holding tanks at each station, usually connected to a cofferdam filled by drains and culverts from the various stopes and drifts behind the dams. Each staging pump forced water up to the next level, where it was eventually discharged outside the mine. They were all connected by long drive rods to a powerful steam-driven pump on the surface.

Normally, the staging pump near each lift shaft was a constant noise they had grown used to and ignored. Now its absence was notable, and it reminded them to be wary of the cofferdam in the neighboring drift and the holding tank that supported the dam. As they passed, water that had accumulated since last week, when the pumps were shut down, was already visibly overflowing the dam spillway into the holding tank, and was mere inches from the tank brim.

To the rest of the crew, it was a typical workday except that it was also their last. Labor that requires little mental exercise becomes monotonous. The only concentration needed was on whatever metal junk was in their hands at the moment. Daylight and cleanliness were too distant to dream about.

Time passed, and later in the day, after the only highlight—lunch—had come and gone, they were all nearly spent. The end of their normal shift had come and gone, and they hoped each load they put on the lift was the last. But there was always one more drift to check, and more gear kept turning up. They all looked forward to the final ride up to clean air and clean clothes.

But to Jack, in addition to the tedious work at hand, it seemed half his head was devoted to his plans for tonight and tomorrow, and what the future held for himself and Jillian. He knew they were long past the time he expected to be done working, but despite the delay, he was starting to believe it might all come together.

He would be free from work to go down to Philipsburg and be there when the station opened in the morning to get a train ticket ahead of time. In fact, he would get two tickets to save time when Jillian arrived, in case they were hurried. He had even secured lodging for the night before, so that time was on his side in the morning. He had full confidence that Jillian would find a means of separating herself from the doctor just long enough so they could make a safe head start. He had already withdrawn his cash from the Hyde-Freychlag Bank and hidden it in his room. The company had even announced that everyone's final wages would be paid out at the end of the last shift, so that extra cash would help even more.

Yes, the plan, like so many plans in so many stories, was destined to succeed.

—

NEAR THE HOIST STATION, AN ITALIAN MINER named Carlo Vinetti wrestled a heavy rock drill up the tunnel toward the lift with another man, Anthony Thompson. The cage had made seven trips to the bottom so far. The day had dragged long over their normal shift, and they hoped Kearney and Fallon and the rest hadn't found any more equipment to send up. The two men struggled and swore as they dragged and pushed the machine to the lift.

As the apparatus teetered on its pedestal beside the nearly full water tank, Thompson paused to change his grip, but it tipped over and crashed sideways into the wooden side of the tank. The impact of the heavy drill body crushed the upper three courses of wooden slats, which were banded together with metal straps and tarred on the inside. The drill paused for a moment at the top band, but gravity took over, and the drill fell further with a thunderous boom, breaking even more slats. Tea-colored water instantly gushed over the broken side of the tank, soaking the two miners.

"What was that?" said Kearney. Far down another drift, he and Jack both heard a faint rumble.

"Whoa, boy. But I don't like it."

They dropped the air hoses they were gathering and started running toward the lift station. They were still hundreds of yards away from the lift when they noticed water running down the floor of the drift toward them. Soon, it was a *lot* of water.

By the time the lights near the lift were in sight far ahead, the water had reached their knees. The rest of the crew came wading up from the drift they had been working in. All of them shouting variations of, "Get to the lift!" and "Get out!"

When they finally reached the shaft, they found Thompson desperately trying to lift the fallen drill off of Vinetti, who was trapped under the rushing water.

Jack wondered where all that water had come from so suddenly, but saw at once that the holding tank had ruptured. In the dim light, he also realized that the holding tank, which was built against the front of the cofferdam, was now nearly empty. Even worse, the cofferdam itself had failed. Once the weight of the tank water was gone from the dam face, it too had let loose, and who knew how many tons of water had collected back in the abandoned drifts and stopes behind it.

He and three other men set about pulling and lifting the heavy machine. Carlo had been held underwater for many minutes now. But the pedestal was entangled with broken slats and bands from the broken dam. It took all of them to clear the wreckage.

Kearney and the others ran to the lift, and Tim began tugging furiously on the bell cord to signal for the cage. A placard next to the lift opening displayed the bell code for their level, plus an emergency code in large red letters at the bottom. Most of the placard was now under the rising water, and Kearney, who had never had reason to read the emergency code, now held his breath and ducked under the stained, cold water long enough to read it quickly and come up gasping for air.

He clung to the side of the hoist frame and yanked on the cord three times, paused, and then three times more. Then he paused again and signaled the level he was at, one-pause-five-pause-five. Then he waited a bit and began the whole sequence over again, forcing himself not to rush and lose count.

The rest of the men on the crew had succeeded in pulling Vinetti from under the drill, but now they were all up to their chins in the flowing torrent. Jack held the man's head above the rising river, and they all crowded around the opening to the lift.

Kearney carefully craned his head over the gate and looked up into the blackness of the shaft, hoping to see the cage coming to save them. He only took a quick look—if the cage suddenly arrived, he would be killed instantly. But it was completely dark up above. None of them could hear anything over the rushing water, so they could only hope rescue was on the way.

33

THE HOIST MAN AT THE TOP OF THE SHAFT HAD one job. He listened for the bell all day long, signaling the cage to be lowered or raised to the level called for. No one spoke to him, nor he to them, mainly so he could concentrate on the bells.

Andre` Lavelle had been with Granite Mining Company for ten years. The first four had been underground until he lost a foot to an ore cart on the tracks at the three-hundred-foot level. He spoke some English, though his vocabulary greatly expanded that day. When he had healed from his wound, management offered him the perfect job for his ability: hoist operator. It was perfect. His English was poor, but that was no problem: he wasn't supposed to speak to anyone. He understood the bell codes, as they were designed for uneducated men. He was far from uneducated, but intelligent and well-suited to the position. He was patient, reliable, and had become adept at maneuvering the cage perfectly to each stop.

Like everyone else, he knew he was out of work at the end of this day, but he was determined to finish the shift with the steady hands he was known for at the controls.

When the bell code sounded next to his station, Andre`
was startled to hear the three-bell emergency call. Every
time he had heard it in his ten years, it was always bad news.
As the bell started clanging, the lift was already on its way
up from the two-hundred-foot level with a load of machinery, so he worked the levers to bring it up even faster. A
group of men in the hoist room heard the emergency signal,
too, and rushed to the lift to clear it off as soon as it arrived.

The cage empty, Andre` immediately sent it speeding
downward to the bottom of the shaft. It took five or six
minutes to lower a cage full of men that far. But since it was
empty, there was no need to be gentle, and the cage plummeted down as fast as the gears would fly.

Jack and most of the crew at the fifteen-hundred-foot
level were now standing on whatever debris they could feel
with their feet to keep their heads above water. The unfortunate Vinetti was held up by four others, but they all knew
he was dead. They only kept hold of him to bring him up
with them.

The Lord's Prayer and many Hail Marys were uttered
several times while they waited and shivered in the faint
glow of one remaining dim Davy light. Thompson said his
in Latin, the only version he knew. The sound of flooding
echoed around them, but the adjoining tunnels were closing
up fast, and the noise diminished somewhat.

They began to hear the clanking of the cage as it neared
the bottom and felt deliverance was at hand. With a splash,
the cage crashed into the water and sank below them with
only a few feet of open space above the gate to climb in.

No one spoke; the expression on each face stolid and
caring for his friends. There was no discussion: those closest

to the gate climbed into the cage, as many as could fit. They had arrived in three groups, but that was in comfort. Half their number clambered inside and squeezed together, each thankful for the warmth of the man next to him.

Kearney grabbed the signal rope and rang for the cage to be lifted again, and it immediately started the long climb.

Then only Jack, Kearney, Clancy, three others, and the lifeless Vinetti remained.

"Five minutes up. Five minutes back down," shivered Jack.

"Aye. But now the 'down' is an express. I won't be stickin' my head in there lookin' for it now," said Kearney, his jaw shuddering just above the cold water.

The sound of the flooding water had decreased as the flow slowed to a gentle stream. Luckily, there were enough empty drifts to hold the flood, so they were no longer in danger of drowning. The cold was bad enough. The wait, torture.

Soon, even the Davy light went out. They prayed some more.

Despite the physical presence of death tugging at all of them, Jack still thought of Jillian. How could they come this close to happiness and have it snatched away by millions of gallons of water? He knew the danger when he took the job, but no one expects the odds to catch up with them. Always someone else.

Vinetti, there. He thought he'd be done today, collect his wages, and look for work again tomorrow. Now he was dead. Jack prayed they lost no one else.

After an eternity—time in the dark seemed to stand still—they heard the faraway clanking of the cage once again. Because the noise had lessened, the sound carried farther, and they heard it long before it finally arrived.

But arrive it did, and they hurriedly dragged Vinetti aboard and piled in together. The dead body extinguished any exuberance at being rescued, though they all inwardly thanked Providence for their survival.

At the surface, the cage squealed to a slow halt, and men crowded around to help them and their deceased friend off. The last shift on any job was to be remembered, but this one would be told and retold many times.

Now that he was safe, Jack's own brush with death hardly affected him. More important matters weighed on his mind. As bad as he felt for Carlo, his thoughts were wholly consumed with how the late ending of his shift would affect his timetable tonight.

34

AS THE LAST SHADES OF EVENING TURNED DARKER toward night, Robert prepared the carriage for their last trip down the mountain. His valise was already in the wagon, the horse was hitched, and he had collected anything he would need on the road, to wherever they would end up.

Earlier in the day, he sold the horse and wagon to John Carmichael of City Stables down in Philipsburg, who would retrieve them at the station after he and Jillian left on the morning train.

In the twilight, Robert could see that traffic on the Philipsburg Road had slowed to nothing. No traffic meant a safer journey in the dark, and no people to see them. He still harbored a dark alternate ending for the evening, but pushed it away, hoping it wouldn't be necessary.

The only thing left now was to wait for Jillian and head down the hill. She was still picking out a few things for her suitcase. *Women have unfathomable logic when it comes to packing for a trip. A few things for a few days. That's all that's necessary.*

His own thoughts revolved around the notion of what to do about his suspicions, but he kept putting the decision off, refusing to consider it.

Once, when he was a boy, he had to get rid of a decomposing possum from under his mother's house. He kept procrastinating because of the distasteful nature of the job ahead, knowing full well that the longer he waited, the more repugnant the task would become.

A final solution had refused to leave his mind in recent days, but this afternoon it had been cemented by a passing comment from one of the orderlies in the hospital shortly after lunch.

Robert had just finished lunch and came downstairs to find Handy Brown, a young Army veteran who served as an orderly, to release him from his employment. Handy already knew his days were numbered, and only hung around after his last payday out of loyalty to the company, even though there were no patients to attend to.

Of their two orderlies, Brandt had always favored Handy. They were both Army veterans, and Handy was always professional, which Brandt respected. But at times, he had a light demeanor, finding humor in grave situations. He was tall and thin and had a big bushy mustache that twitched back and forth when he was being mischievous, but sometimes his jokes fell flat.

Brandt met him in the hallway. "Handy, you know we're finished here."

"Yes, sir. Sad to see the mine fold like this. I'm glad I'm not a miner."

"Yes. Well, Mrs. Brandt and I are leaving this evening for town down below. I've no further work for you here, so you are released from any obligations to the hospital as of now."

"I understand, Doctor. It's just that, well, I've nowhere else to be. I suppose I'll head down in the morning myself and see what comes next."

"That's fine." They shook hands. "Goodbye, Handy."

"Goodbye, Doctor Brandt. Good luck."

Everything might have been fine, but as they parted, Handy had a lopsided grin. "I guess you'll be glad to put some miles between that young miner and y'all."

"What?" Brandt said icily.

"I'm sorry, sir. Didn't mean nothing by it. Just silly people talkin', ya know?"

He felt he was overstepping, so he shut up. Handy took a step or two back.

"Anyway. Good luck, sir."

Handy made a hasty exit down the hall and disappeared.

Brandt could feel the pounding in his head. People were talking? He was a laughingstock. They must think he's running away and taking his wandering wife to keep her out of trouble.

It took him longer to calm down this time. Perhaps making the decision about what to do—once and for all— helped his blood pressure come back down. He had been quiet all through dinner, but she didn't seem to notice, or wasn't interested enough in his mood to ask.

Now it was time to leave, and she was still dawdling about upstairs, attending to useless details. He fought to control himself. She shouldn't see his anger. It might alarm her and make the trip difficult, so he pushed it down deep.

As he turned away from the wagon to look for her, Jillian came out onto the receiving porch with her suitcase in hand.

"Are we ready?" she said casually. "If you have someone taking care of the house things, I have a few days' things packed in my bag, as you asked."

She seemed in a light mood, even upbeat, but he knew she had to be thinking of that boy. If she was so ready to leave now, there must be something afoot.

"Yes." There was no smile in his voice. "Let's be off."

He placed her bag in the back of the wagon, but didn't even offer to help her up. Not that she needed it. She had driven the carriage many times to town by herself. But she did think it odd. Even when they were on the outs, he had outwardly been a gentleman.

Robert hopped up on the seat and unhooked the reins. As soon as she was seated, he released the hand brake and they rode off.

35

THE ROAD FROM GRANITE DOWN TO PHILIPSBURG wound down the mountainside with few intersecting trails. A short distance downhill from the hospital, it passed the working yards of another mine called the Blaine Shaft, part of the Bi-Metallic Mining Company holdings, which descended 1,800 feet under the Earth. The headframe and hoist house lay a short distance off the road, and like most of the local works, it too had shut down with the plunge in silver prices.

As their carriage rounded a bend in the road, Robert slowed and leaned over the side, peering through the darkness toward the headframe. The dark, creosoted timbers were nearly invisible in the gloom.

Jillian couldn't see what he was looking at.

"What's wrong?" she asked.

"Someone has left the shaft gate open. I don't see anyone around."

He pulled up at the yard entrance, set the brake on the wagon, and climbed down.

"I'm going to close the gate, but it takes two people. Climb down and help me?"

She craned her neck and tried to pierce the darkness.

"How can you even see it from here?"

"Jillian!" He softened his voice so she wouldn't be on the defensive. "Please."

She knew he was determined, so she climbed out of the wagon, though she could hardly see the headframe over the shaft, let alone any kind of gate. He took her hand and led her through the mine yard. She still could not see the gate, but the headframe towered above them, blanking out stars as they walked.

As they got closer, Robert's grip on her arm tightened to the point where it became painful.

"Robert, you're hurting me."

He pulled her close to him and took her shoulders in his strong hands.

"As you have hurt me?"

She drew in a quick breath. His face was close to hers, and even in the starlight, she could see his eyes glowering in anger.

"Yes, Jillian. I know. I've known all along."

"What are you talking about—"

He shook her, and her head rocked back and forth.

"You've embarrassed me in the town," he said. "You and that Irish ruffian. People are talking about us. About you. I won't have it."

Panic grew in the pit of her stomach.

"Robert, I swear to you, there is nothing to talk about. We're leaving now anyway, isn't that so? Whatever you've heard, whatever people have said, there's nothing! I love—"

"Don't you dare speak of love!" he hissed. "I've loved you and provided for you, and now you've become infatuated with this man. For no other reason than that he has filled your head with fantasies."

They stood in front of the open gate to the mine shaft, and it finally dawned on her that he must have planned this ahead of time. No one had left the gate open. Earlier today, when he rode to Philipsburg to sell their horse and wagon, he probably came here and opened this iron gate himself.

"Robert, please…"

Despite the swings of life from good times to bad, and back again, that dark part of him that he had battled for so many years had won out. He leaned closer to her face, his voice almost a whisper.

"He will not have you. Nor you him. And not anyone."

It took almost no force at all, but in one short moment, all his weight went to her shoulders as he spun her around and pushed.

Jillian let out only a short, surprised yelp and disappeared down into the black, open maw of the mine shaft.

She felt her body turn, and in that moment, his grip was so strong. At first, she thought he only meant to frighten her. But then he let go, and she felt nothing under her feet. Her body seemed to float for a moment. When she took a step, there was nothing underfoot. She started to scream, but the wind in her face was like a cold breath of death. Down, down, falling into the blackest pitch imaginable. Her arms flailed, her coat flapped in the air faster and faster.

Once or twice, she saw the opening to the sky and stars swirling above, but soon even that disappeared in darkness.

—

ROBERT STOOD FROZEN FOR SEVERAL MOMENTS, shock rooting him to the ground. His breathing and his anger slackened, and the realization of what he had just done came to him. Two sides of his psyche fighting over his soul.

He never heard the impact of her body at the bottom of the shaft. But then, it was a third of a mile down.

Fully surrendering to the moment, the proud doctor swung the shaft gate closed and threw the latch. Easy enough for one man to tidy up.

"There," he said to himself. "All safe and shut. Very careless. Someone might have fallen in."

He wiped the rust of the gate from his hands as he walked back to the wagon. Releasing the brake, he click-clicked the horse to continue down the road to Philipsburg.

36

AFTER THE TRAGIC ENDING OF THE LAST SHIFT, their shift boss finally told them to leave whatever was left down the hole and be done.

Twenty-six men were left standing around the hoist room after Vinetti's body had been taken down to the hospital morgue. Those who had managed to escape drowning were soaking wet and muddy. The others who had helped from the topside remained in camaraderie while they all talked themselves down from the adrenaline charging their bodies.

"I thought we were dead," said Jack.

"Me, too," said another.

"Some of us were," Jack finished.

They all muttered "Ay" in agreement.

Kearney, wiping mud from his face, said what a few others were thinking, "It's good this thing is shut down. I'm done with minin'." But he was just blowing off steam. He knew he had no other skills and would be back underground at the next job.

Thompson had been mostly quiet since he left the cage.

He finally spoke up, "If I hadn't lost my grip..." He stopped there and lost his voice.

Jack put a hand on his shoulder. "This wasn't your fault, Anthony. It's nobody's fault. We're all tired, and it could be any of us who lost his grip, or be lyin' there dead."

It was Red Clancy who broke the somber tone. "Boys, I never saw Jack get so cozy with a stiff 'til he climbed in that cage with Carlo!"

The entire room burst into laughter.

Brownlow let them all talk it out, and then, once the mood finally lightened, told them all to report to the company office to draw their final wages.

"You men have been a fine bunch to work with at any mine. I'm sorry the last shift ended up like this, but just remember the good times we had. Good luck to you all."

At that, he turned and left. Those closest to him later swore they heard him sniffle.

Jack's shift would normally have ended at 4 p.m., but with so much work plus the final bit of tragedy, it was just after 9 o'clock when he finally tagged out.

When their shift ended, Jack and his coworkers visited The Dry to clean up a bit before rejoining the public. Most had already made plans to leave town and were slow to say goodbye to their friends, knowing this was one of the last times they would all be together. After the accident, they agreed this would also be the wake for Vinetti, even though the guest of honor would not be present. Rents were paid up, and traveling plans made; they couldn't wait for the undertaker.

As they left, Tim Kearney and Clancy buttonholed Jack as he turned toward his room.

"Hold up, there, Jack. We've one more job to do." Kearney held up a length of rope with a mischievous grin.

Clancy looked around to make sure no one was close.

Jack had no interest in hijinx. He knew only that he had to find Jillian somehow and make their way to the train station, but his curiosity was piqued.

"Tim, I'm tired and not interested in any more jobs tonight. But okay, what's the rope for?"

"This company is done. The mine is done. There'll be no more shifts for anyone. That steam whistle is the bane of our working life, Jack-O. We're gonna tie her off and let the whole town mourn the passing of the once-great Granite Mining Company."

"You're crazy. And you'll get… fired." He caught himself. *We're all fired anyway.* "But you go have your fun."

They laughed and invited Jack to join them at Rosemary's for a final going-away party. Jack told them he might be along later as he had a few things to take care of before retiring for the night.

If they could just get started, without interruption from the already suspicious doctor, Jack was sure they could escape. He only hoped Han had delivered his note and that she could at least avoid her husband long enough to find her way down to Philipsburg. He would either intercept her tonight or find her down at the train station tomorrow, but he had to be ready either way.

Jack stopped by Headley's boarding house and stuffed what few possessions he had into his travel sack. A few clothes, his razor, and some sundries, which fit with room to spare. Until he fished around under his mattress for his poke, the cash withdrawal he had made at the bank. Stuffing the bills tightly wrapped in butcher's paper into the bottom of his bag, he cinched up the straps and took a last look around the room. His lodging was paid up until the end of the week, and no one was around at this late hour to say goodbye. The lamp in Mrs. Headley's room was dark. He snuffed out his own lamp, closed the door, walked down the stairs, and out to the street.

The last rays of the sun had long departed, and the sky was a deep purple. The hospital sat dark and seemingly deserted at the top of the road down to Philipsburg. Jack cut between the Catholic church and the Methodist church to the shadowed side of the hospital, where he could see the receiving doors at the back. He stood in the gathering gloom, hoping to see some light upstairs in the Doctor's and Jillian's apartment above.

Suddenly, the steam whistle at the mine let loose its loud, shrill wail. Jack nearly jumped out of his skin.

Three times every day, that whistle signaled the start of another shift. It was loud enough to be heard all over town— designed to be loud enough to wake an errant miner from a late, drunken sleep. It usually sounded for twenty or thirty seconds and then stopped. But tonight, the long, moaning blast went on and on, like a final, long dying breath.

It took almost an hour to bleed down the steam left in the boiler. By the time it stopped, Kearney and Clancy were ensconced in their favorite chairs at Rosemary's, raising a sad glass with their friends—to sad Vinetti, to the dying whistle, the dying company, and their dying jobs.

Jack was still skulking around the dark street across from the hospital, patient but anxious.

AS BRANDT STARTED DOWNHILL IN THE DARK, THE only sound came from the crunching of the gravel road under the wagon wheels. Suddenly, he was startled to hear the steam whistle at the mine let out its mournful shriek. The whistle had gone silent in recent days, there being only one shift in operation. His first, subconscious thought was that it was Jillian's last cry from the mine shaft, but he immediately dismissed the possibility. Yet the idea took root and haunted him all the way down the mountainside. Between the memory of the sudden whistle sounding in the night and the occasional brief squeal of the wagon's rear axle, or the squeak of the springs under his seat, Robert's mind heard only his wife's last cry as she fell.

He eventually rounded the last curve in the road, nearing the town, and was glad to be far away from the life he had left up in Granite—and the life he had ended there. He thought better of boarding the train in Philipsburg; he might be recognized, and questions about his wife would surely follow. Better to drive all the way to Drummond in the dark and then catch a train to somewhere far westward. It was a twenty-five-mile ride in full darkness, but the road was mostly straight with few turnoffs. There was no risk of getting lost, and less risk of encountering anyone. He would leave the carriage and horse in Drummond, with instructions to the station manager to get word to John Carmichael to come and collect them.

All his loose ends were tidied up. Nothing to hold him. Robert Brandt drove on into the night.

The next morning, he boarded the westbound Northern Pacific and was gone.

———

JACK HAD DISCREETLY OBSERVED ALL SIDES OF the hospital for some time and decided no one was coming or going. Not too surprising for the time of night, but he had hoped she might have found the opportunity to slip out so they could make their way together down to the town below.

Either she had already gone, or she would leave early in the morning to get away. In any event, he decided to go down to Philipsburg and wait there until she showed up. It would be a long, chilly walk down the mountain in the middle of the night, but his dreams of a future with Jillian would keep him warm inside.

37

The Missoulian, September 4, 1893

TERRIBLE TRAIN WRECK

Westbound Pullman Cars Leave Tracks

Missoula, Sept 4—The westbound train from Drummond to Missoula jumped the tracks near Quigley on Saturday last, causing three cars to derail, with one rolling down an embankment into the rushing Blackfoot River. Officials of the Northern Pacific Railroad tell of considerable damage to four of the six cars on the route that day. All the passengers and crew on board, save one, are safe and sound, albeit some with dreadful injuries.

One unfortunate occupant was nearly thrown clear of the Pullman car that ended on its side in the Blackfoot, but, sadly, was killed. It is generally believed by all involved that the survival of the remaining passengers was an act of Providence.

THE TRAIN CONSISTED OF AN ENGINE, OF COURSE, and a coal car, plus one freight car and three passenger cars. The dreadful crash was reported in the Missoulian newspaper the following week. On board were the engineer, the fireman, the conductor, and twenty-six passengers. All survived except one. The conductor described him as a dark-haired man of about 40 years, traveling alone. He had boarded in Drummond with only two hand-carried bags and a ticket for Spokane.

The conductor and the few passengers who could recall after such a traumatic event said that the man chose to sit alone in the rearmost car. The other passengers, as travelers do, spread themselves generally throughout the other two cars, and the trip was otherwise uneventful.

For one reason or another, the speed of the train was slightly greater than usual, probably owing to the fewer-than-typical number of cars. As the train rounded a curve, the heavy engine and coal cars tipped up on the rails just far enough to cause the other cars to derail. The third car became detached and rolled into the river, ending up on its side.

The survivors counted their blessings as they took stock of their own injuries. Help came down from Quigley, and they were all taken to the small town to see to their injuries.

It wasn't until the conductor—whose leg was broken—was able to get an accurate count of who was present at the little church in Quigley, the only building big enough to hold so many people, that he realized one was missing: the loner in the third car.

The next morning—despite it being Sunday—work crews arrived by rail from Missoula to start cleaning up the mess. With the rails blocked, the Sabbath had to take a back seat. The work train they brought had a crane car to lift the partially submerged passenger car back onto the tracks.

It took a good part of the morning to rig cables and blocks to begin hoisting the flooded car out of the river. As it hung suspended above the surface, the crew paused to allow water to drain from the coach. It was only then that the last passenger was found.

It was surmised that as the car was rolling down the embankment, he had nearly been thrown out the window nearest his seat. He was almost clear, but both his legs were still inside the car as it came to rest, and he was trapped only inches below the surface of the cold river. His last moments before drowning must have been in excruciating pain.

He had no identification papers on his person, but one of the suitcases he boarded with contained a doctor's bag and medical tools. Officials assumed he was some kind of travelling physician.

The county sheriff was summoned because of the fatality, but the cause of death was obviously due to the train accident, and the case was closed without further investigation. The body was buried locally.

38

VOICES ARGUED LOUDLY IN THE ROOM ABOVE AS Jack opened one eye at a time to begin the day he hoped would be his last in Philipsburg. He was in the basement of the laundry business owned by Han's uncle, Tom Yen. He had gratefully accepted the room for a night or two in his belief that his stay would be very short. It was comfortable enough for one or two nights, but he was glad it wasn't his permanent residence. He hoped the arguing he heard wasn't over his presence in the house.

The arguing voices of the family upstairs grew louder, and then it sounded like furniture was being rearranged. His Chinese neighbors apparently were starting today as they started every day, arguing about something or other. Finally, the front door slammed, and a bit of dust falling from the rafters caught the sunlight from a small window in Jack's room.

The plan was to meet Jillian in the vicinity of the train station if they missed each other on Friday night, so Jack decided to stay in Philipsburg and try to find her. To save time, he purchased two tickets on the 12 o'clock Northern Pacific train bound for Drummond.

Jillian had not appeared on Friday night, so Jack waited at the station the following day. Again, she did not show up, so he resolved to be at the station again today, and every day until she came, in case she had been delayed by her husband. He was certain she would come at some point. With Granite emptying out, people were leaving every day, and Jack knew the doctor would have seen the futility of staying behind with no one needing doctoring. But if they failed to find each other much longer, he would have to find a short-term job somewhere so he could eat. It was important that he avoid dipping into his savings if he could avoid it. If he and Jillian were to have any chance at a life together, he would need every penny to see them through until he found profitable work.

A miner's wife was not in the cards for Jillian, if he could help it. He wanted a much better life for her than she had known, and surely the wife of a miner was a step down from her present station. So he accepted the challenge ahead, vowing to do anything he could to improve her life. They would have to live simply until the Green Isle became a reality, but he was certain they would succeed. He couldn't wait to share his plan with her for the finest saloon in the country. Surely she would see that they would not be living in poverty.

He rose and dressed, emptied the pitcher on the nightstand into a bowl, and washed up. If Jillian did not show up today, he might have to risk returning to Granite and perhaps the hospital, too, to find her. He hoped that would not be necessary.

As presentable as he could make himself, he picked up his worn traveling bag and walked out into the morning.

It was less than a half-mile walk to the railroad station, and he took a position on the waiting bench outside, where he could see if Jillian or anyone else approached the station from town.

The station manager, Elliston Booker, had worked for the Northern Pacific as a station manager for eleven years, all of them right here in Philipsburg. He knew almost everyone who came and went from the town: bankers and freighters, ranchers, and restaurateurs—all having need of the railroad at some point. Some of them he had known all his life; others he had observed getting off the train from elsewhere to begin a new life here or seek riches in the mines above town. Some of the latter he had also seen leaving after a few years, brokenhearted from trying hard but losing everything.

Men came full of hope and dreamed of striking a good vein on their own, only to slowly drain away the meager savings they had brought with them, and eventually be forced to work for someone else. When they had again put aside enough to move on, they did so. These were the people Elliston recognized on their way out. They had a look of defeat or resentment, and wanted only to be away from this place that had crushed their dream.

The young man sitting on the bench at the end of the platform was just such a man, with that same look—though not quite. Elliston remembered the fellow getting off the train the previous spring. *Irish*, thought Elliston at the time, though neither had spoken to the other. *He had a look. Cocky and clean, but tough, and that little snap-brim cap the Irish wore.* He had seen him again when he brought a telegram to be sent from the Granite company a few weeks prior.

And now he was back. The man bought two tickets from Elliston for the Spokane routing the day before, and seemed anxious about something. Now he had returned, and still had that expectant look about him, even more worried than the day before.

But people come and people go around here, and Elliston kept his judgments to himself. He imagined the second ticket was possibly meant for a lady friend and, since he knew most, if not all, the people in town, Elliston was a little curious himself to see who it might be. If she came at all. The man had waited around for the train yesterday, too. Still, no judgments to be made.

Late in the day, after the train had come and gone again, Jack walked up to the ticket window in the station.

"Excuse me, sir," said Jack. "If you remember, I purchased some tickets yesterday…"

Elliston glanced up from his freight schedules and looked over his spectacles at Jack.

"Oh yes, son, of course I remember," Booker said. "This little station, it ain't Butte." He chuckled at his own joke.

"Yes, well, I was wondering, would you know if someone came here yesterday?" Jack searched for words. "After I left, I mean, looking for another train maybe?"

"Sorry, no. I remember you were waiting here all afternoon after the Drummond train left. But you see, there is only the one train, no other trains afterward." He smiled and said again, "This ain't Butte."

Jack nodded. "I understand. It's just that, well, if someone were to come around looking to meet someone and they missed them…"

"Nope. No one came down here to the station later in the day."

Elliston felt for the man. It was obvious he was worried his friend hadn't arrived.

"I've worked here for many years, son, and I know everybody around here. Perhaps if I knew who it was you were expecting, I could keep an eye open for, uh, for them?"

"That's alright. I think I'll go and look around town. Thank you, though."

Jack touched his brimmed cap and slowly walked off the platform in the direction of town.

It was impossible for Jack to admit he was planning to run away with a married woman, let alone a prominent wife of the town doctor up at Granite. He would just have to hope for the best and keep his secret to himself.

He repeated this same short act for many days, each time with the same or similar dialogue, and the same unresolved ending.

When Jack ran low on money, he took work at one of the smaller mines above Philipsburg. He earned enough to eat, and Han's uncle still refused any reasonable remuneration for his room at the Chinese laundry.

He worked as many days as he could, but whenever he was between short jobs or had a full day off to himself, he would always check in at the station.

Caution finally gave way to desperation, and he walked the four miles up to Granite. The tram was no longer in use, and empty ore buckets hung motionless along the cable. No carts or wagons passed him going up the hill. One came down, though, loaded down with the driver's belongings, an older man whom Jack remembered as one of the shopkeepers in Granite. Cigars and tobacco, as he recalled, next door to the Ruby Hotel.

Jack stopped beside the road, and the man paused.

"I hope you're not looking for work up that hill, sonny," the man said. "No one up there but ghosts."

"No, sir, I know. The mine closed. Is anyone left in the town?"

"Not many, no. Just about all of them gone to the four winds. None of the shops are left, either."

"Well, maybe I'll see someone I know."

"Maybe. You take care."

The man clicked his horse and rode downhill. Jack continued on to Granite.

His first stop was the hospital, of course. No sense trying to be stealthy now.

The door stood wide open, and a slow breeze wafted out as he climbed the steps and entered.

There is a sound an empty building makes, less heard than felt. It's not a note or a creaking, not even the sigh of wind through vacant halls. Just the sense of no living soul within. Jack stood in the front hall and listened to the emptiness. No one was there, nor had anyone been for some time.

He roamed the main roads around the town and passed a handful of residents, all spread out, some in the commercial area, but most in the residential neighborhoods, hardcore loners who refused to give up. He recognized a few, but spoke to no one.

The Union Hall was empty as well. Wandering through the ground floor, he remembered the music and the dancing that used to shake the building to its timbers. Someone once told him the floor was specially built with springy wood just made for dancing. Now, everything had a layer of dust.

He was tempted to go up to the mine works, but why bother? Jillian wouldn't be up in that neighborhood, even if she was still in the town somewhere.

Nothing he saw around the town changed his first impression when he had walked into the empty hospital hallway. She was gone. Gone with thousands of others who had fled the sinking ship of Granite.

He didn't feel she had abandoned him by any means. When they last spoke, they were absolutely sure of their path forward. Deep inside, he could still feel she wanted to be with him, that she must be close by. But he could think of nowhere else to look.

Hands in his pockets, he headed back down the hill. Another menial job awaited him the next day.

He had been knocking around Philipsburg for a few weeks now and had seen nothing of her or the doctor there. He kept his ears open, too, and overheard no conversations about the doctor coming down from Granite to work in the lower town.

Even Han and his family had abandoned their business up on the mountain and moved into the building above Jack's room. No doubt it was the crowded living conditions between the two families trying to adjust to their new situation that kept the argument alive every morning.

Jack asked Han many times if he had seen Jillian either up at Granite or during his travels about Philipsburg, but he had nothing to report.

The weeks grew into months, and still Jillian did not come to him at the railroad station. He never found her or heard a word about either of them around town.

The more he considered her failure to meet him, the more he realized she really may have changed her mind. Decided not to go on the run with a lowly miner.

Of course, that was it.

He had been fooling himself to think he could have tempted a lady like Jillian away from a comfortable life as a doctor's wife. If she was unhappy, as he could clearly see she was, it was still preferable to whatever kind of existence she must have thought he could provide for her.

On the other hand, what if Brandt had discovered their elopement? What if he had forced her to tell him what that plan was?

Jack dismissed that possibility, as the good doctor had not come hunting for him. As sure as he was that he loved Jillian, he was equally sure that her husband loved her also, as misshapen as that kind of love was, that it could allow a man to mistreat his own wife so.

In any case, he knew the doctor's temper would have driven him to find and "deal" with Jack in such a way that he would either be back in the hospital, or taken up permanent residence in the town cemetery.

Thoughts such as these roamed around Jack's head over that entire winter. He worked, ate, slept, and kept to himself in a quiet, lonely life.

And any day he had time between jobs, he walked to the train station and waited for the noon train, watching everyone who came and went.

39

AFTER THE FLOOD OF PEOPLE FROM GRANITE slowed, the passage of winter in Philipsburg crept along at its typical frozen pace. Winters in Montana are always challenging, especially nearly a mile above sea level. Snow comes early and stays late, and businesses always need help clearing it away to remain open. Easy earnings for Jack.

His landlord refused to take any rent for the first few months, but eventually, Jack convinced Han's uncle to accept what he believed was a fair rate for a room with a little heat and a good roof. No extra charge for the daily wake-up call of shouting upstairs.

Han Liu and his parents and brothers eventually moved on like the rest of the citizens of Granite. Han told Jack they were going to try a new venture in Butte. Apparently, his ever-quarrelling relatives were too cantankerous even for them.

Winter thawed into spring, and summer bloomed up on the mountain. The few holdouts who had refused to leave the previous autumn finally accepted the town's fate, and they, too, picked up stakes and moved away.

Jack kept busy at various smaller mines, and the hard work kept his mind off what might have been. The empty echoes inside him felt like the vacant hospital that day he had returned to Granite.

He and Jillian had barely had time to even consider what a future might have been like. How they might build The Green Isle together. All their thoughts had been spent planning the first few steps on the road to a new life.

He had made his commitment to this woman who, he believed, had brought him back from the brink of death. That he had begun to see some meager reflection of his own feelings back toward him only convinced him that, whatever happened, his life would only be complete if they shared a life together.

Seasons rolled by, and then years.

In 1918, a pair of brothers, named Morris and Humphrey Courtney, bought the land on which Tom Yen's Chinese laundry and Jack's boarding room lay, and Jack had to move again. This time to a dusty but warm room in the back of John Carmichael's livery stables.

Unbeknownst to Jack, it was the same Carmichael who had purchased Doctor Brandt's horse and wagon that fateful night. Jack spent little time at the livery, working at other jobs, so he had little contact or conversation with Mr. Carmichael, in which he might have learned that an important clue to Jillian's disappearance was right there in the same building with him.

Money from the Courtneys' mining interests built a three-story hotel on the land once occupied by the laundry, and, of course, they named it the Courtney Hotel. Each room had its own sink and a window, and steam heat. Two communal baths served each floor. It was a fine place—all very modern. Good hotels were more residential than those meant for travelers. Teachers and lawyers came to live there on a long-term basis, as did a certain Irish miner, no longer young.

Jack's room was on the second floor facing Sansone Street, a location he had asked for so he could watch as people passed by on the street. It was the route one might take coming from, say, Granite down to Philipsburg.

Eventually, he gave up his vigil at the train station, but Jack spent his days and evenings sitting at the window in his room. Oh, he made friends here and there, but none as close as his mates up at Granite back in the old days.

He gave up on Faro and never gambled again. His dream of the Green Isle Saloon also faded. With no one to share an exciting and profitable life as a successful businessman, he slowly lost interest in accumulating extra wealth and was content to make enough to live on and no more.

As the valley economy turned away from mining toward ranching, Jack's age steered him away from heavy mining work, too. In haying season, he could always pick up work, for slinging hay up on a beaver slide was still easier than slinging raw ore into a mine cart a thousand feet underground. Eventually, he sought even less strenuous work as years of hard labor took their toll. Life was winding down like a watch, and he spent more days at his window, more from habit now than any expectation of Jillian's appearance.

The proprietor of the hotel was kind enough to find light janitorial tasks for Jack to do in exchange for part of his rent. The balance forgiven as kindness.

———

IN THE SUMMER OF 1939, LATE ONE AFTERNOON, Frank Horrigan, the proprietor of the Philipsburg Opera House, across the street from the hotel, was changing the marquee out front when he noticed a man slumped over in a window on the second floor of the hotel, his head tilted at an uncomfortably odd angle.

The theater owner went into the hotel and told the desk clerk of the scene in the window, and they both returned to the street and looked up.

The desk clerk sighed, as if he were not at all surprised. He thanked Horrigan, returned to his desk, and immediately phoned Sheriff Angus MacDonald. He asked the sheriff to be present when he went upstairs to check on one of his longtime and oldest residents.

The sheriff's office being only a few blocks away, Angus arrived by automobile in short order. Horses and wagons had almost disappeared, but traffic was still mixed. It was a ranching community, after all, and horses still had many uses.

The sheriff and the clerk mounted the stairs to the second floor, and the clerk used his key to open the door to room 206.

The apartment was tidy, as older gentlemen usually are when living alone. A few clothes hung in the closet. The dresser contained some other clothes, and the top was neatly arranged with the room key marked 206, a man's billfold containing a Granite Miners' Union membership card, and eleven dollars. And a time-worn snap-brimmed cap.

On a worn but comfortable, stuffed chair by the window, with a good view of Sansone Street, sat a man about 70 years old, quite dead.

The desk clerk confirmed the identity, matching the Miners' Union card as that of Mr. Jack Fallon, formerly of Granite before the Crash of '93. Sheriff MacDonald surmised the cause of death to be natural, there being no signs of foul play, and because the gentleman was obviously quite old. The undertaker from Ward's Funeral Parlor down on Broadway was summoned to collect the body.

The undertaker from Ward's placed the remains on hold in a cold storage locker in the basement of the mortuary. An obituary notice appeared in the next edition of the Philipsburg Mail newspaper, announcing the death, in hopes that someone might claim the body and see to the expenses of a proper burial. Although many of Jack's acquaintances called on the funeral home to pay their respects on the day of visitation, none had any inclination, nor felt an obligation, to pay anything more.

And so, after a week in the basement of the funeral home, Jack was taken up to the Philipsburg Cemetery and laid to rest at the expense of the town. No headstone was erected to his memory, only a wooden plank with the plot number. No one attended the burial, as it was during the work week.

Jack left town just as he had arrived all those years ago. Alone.

Epilogue

RALPH, THE MUSEUM DOCENT, SAT BACK IN HIS chair, his last cup of tea long cold.

"And that, my friends," he said, "is the story of Jack Fallon, the man you saw in our upstairs window. Once a miner and now a permanent resident of this hotel."

Janie looked heartbroken. "That's so sad. They never found each other."

"Good story, though," said Steve, still skeptical.

Janie perked up. "Oh, but it's like the nursery rhyme—'Jack and Jill went up the hill, to fetch a pail of water…'"

Ralph looked at her somberly. "But only one came down, I'm afraid."

They stood up and shook hands all around.

"Well, thanks for stopping by," Ralph said. "Enjoy the rest of our town. Take a run up to Granite tomorrow if you have time. It's just up the hillside above town here." He raised his eyebrows and smiled. "It'll probably all look familiar to you now."

Steve was still not sure if he'd been had. "We might just do that. And thank you for a nice afternoon ghost story."

"You bet. Tell Charlene at the candy store you saw him. She'll be so jealous." Ralph waved as they walked out to the street.

Once outside, Steve and Janie looked up again at the window, but it was empty. No sign of any ghosts.

"Do you believe him, Dad?"

"I dunno, honey. This is a touristy town. It could be a bit of folklore meant to draw visitors." They turned and walked downhill toward Broadway, which was busy with out-of-towners exploring the shops.

"Still…" said Steve. "That was a pretty good yarn. We should take a look at that ghost town tomorrow. Alright, so what's next?"

"The candy store!"

"You got it, kiddo."

Afterword

IN 2016, THE CONESTOGA MINING COMPANY—THE current owner of the property that encompasses Granite Ghost Town, and the surrounding mining claims, including the Blaine Shaft—installed a cement cap at the top of the Blaine, just in case silver prices someday improved to the point where reopening the mine would be profitable again.

The massive wooden headframe suspending the mine elevators above the shaft had collapsed a few years before, and, while the mine was clearly marked as private property, tourists en route to the ghost town further uphill frequently veered off the road to explore the Blaine mine yard property. A very dangerous detour, since the headframe was now in ruins and the open shaft was exposed.

The Bertolli family, who owned the Conestoga company, worried about the liability of someone falling to their death in the shaft or damaging some of the old hoist equipment. The hoist house was still there, and several of the old shaft elevator cages were strewn about. Such historic implements of old mining days were highly sought after by collectors, and the mine yard had only a simple metal frame gate to keep vehicles out. The old, rusty iron elevator cages were much too heavy for one or two people to move, but a determined few with a truck and winch could make off with some rare bits of history. Some probably already had.

So it was decided to clean up the yard and cap the shaft. The tilting, thick wooden timbers of the headframe that remained were pulled down and hauled away, and work was begun on the shaft collar to create a support framework for the cement cap.

But first, the debris had to be cleared from down in the shaft itself. A temporary frame and hoist were built, and a work crew descended the 1,800 feet for the first time in over a hundred years.

When they reached the bottom, they were shocked to discover human remains. Apparently, a woman, judging by the clothing. The county sheriff's department was called, and a full investigation was started.

It was immediately apparent that this was no recent event. The clothing and shoes were later dated to the 1890s. The woman wore a high button-up shoes and long coat, called a duster in the old days. In one pocket was a small women's clutch purse containing twenty-three dollars in paper money, fifty-three cents in coins, and a small comb. In the other pocket were a handkerchief and a blank laundry ticket. On the back of the laundry ticket were the handwritten words, "*Wait for me. J.*"

The woman was never identified.

Acknowledgments

THIS BOOK STARTED AS A SIMPLE ANECDOTE AND grew into a living thing. But it could not have come to life without the guidance, skill, and encouragement of several remarkable people.

My heartfelt thanks go to Nathan Bransford, whose editorial insight and patience helped shape this story into its best form. I'm equally grateful to Danna Mathias Steele, whose creative vision and design sense brought the book's interior and cover to life with stunning care and detail.

TJ Vietor, my "partner in time" at Granite County Museum & Cultural Center, thank you for enjoying the tale from the beginning, when it was still in its barest bones. Dave Letford, you are my physical model for one of the early characters—you'll recognize yourself right away, even if no one else does. Thanks for getting me involved in the museum all those years ago.

To my wife, Cindy, who first suggested I "go for it" and who lent an attentive ear along the way, thank you for your patience when I probably talked too much about this project. Thank you for believing in it, and in me.

For all those who enjoy exploring history and take the time to read this, you have my deepest appreciation.

226

About the Author

RICK MCGILL IS A NATIVE OF MARYLAND, WHERE he retired from law enforcement in 2001 before settling in rural Montana. When his quiet retirement was unexpectedly interrupted by the Global War on Terror, he served overseas for six years as a security contractor for the U.S. government in Iraq and elsewhere.

Rick was an active member of the Granite County Museum & Cultural Center board of directors in Philipsburg, Montana. He spent five years developing exhibits at the museum and contributing hands-on restoration work at the museum and at Granite Ghost Town, helping to uncover and protect the region's history. He enjoys Montana's wild landscapes and often ventures onto backcountry trails in search of forgotten relics of the past.

ALSO BY RICK MCGILL:

"Brass Buttons & Gun Leather:
A History of the Laurel Police Department"
4th printing coming soon.

"We Had a Guy"
Coming soon.

"Rediscovering the North Tract:
An Anne Arundel Time Capsule"
Out of print.

www.ingramcontent.com/pod-product-compliance
Lightning Source LLC
Chambersburg PA
CBHW060305310726
48976CB00007B/2220